It was the kind of kiss that Cordelia remembered sharing with Paul the last time she saw him—on the steps of her house back in San Diego. A part of her wished she could go back in time and stay on the steps with Paul forever. But as Paul kissed her, she knew that they couldn't be that way again. She suddenly knew who she wished she could kiss—someone completely off-limits.

GETTING LOST WITH BOYS

Hailey ABBOTT

AVON BOOKS

An Imprint of HarperCollins*Publishers*

www.harperteen.com

 Produced by Alloy Entertainment
151 West 26th Street, New York, NY 10001
Library of Congress Catalog Card number: 2005906570
ISBN-10: 0-06-082432-8 – ISBN-13: 978-0-06-082432-7
Typography by Joel Tippie
❖
First Avon edition, 2006

Chapter One

Cordelia Packer was the most uncomfortable she'd ever been. More uncomfortable than when she'd contracted the chicken pox from Alexis Dunbar, her best friend, in kindergarten. More uncomfortable than when she'd puked up her hot dog lunch onto Alexis's shoes during the semifinal round of the fifth-grade spelling bee after being asked to spell "forsythia." Actually, now that Cordelia thought about it, she was experiencing the most uncomfortable moment of her life, and Alexis was nowhere to be found. Weird. She wished she could call Alexis now.

But even weirder was the fact that she was out here *camping*. Cordelia never slept on anything except a queen-size bed fitted with two layers of four-hundred–thread-count sheets and a goose down comforter. Now she was lying on the floor of a tent that smelled like wet canvas, trying to reach the stone that had been digging into her back all night. This stone had single-handedly ruined the restful sleep that she had planned, and it was currently threatening to ruin something that could have been etched in her mind as the most incredible moment of all time, instead of the most uncomfortable. That certain something was the full-on, hip-grinding make-out session she was having with her exceptionally wonderful and gorgeous boyfriend, Paul.

Not only was Paul seriously sexy, he also had a way of convincing Cordelia to put aside her slightly rigid quality-of-life requirements. This time, he had won her over with the fact that Torrey Pines State Reserve was located near the beach. Cordelia hadn't heard the word *near*—only the word *beach*. Cordelia always considered the beach to be her second home—she just loved listening to the roaring sound of the ocean waves. But instead of relaxing in the sand, she was nestled in a tepee-like contraption and surrounded by a forest of pine trees. Not exactly what she'd had in mind.

But she tried to refocus her thoughts on the good stuff, like how Paul was now kissing the length of her neck. God, Paul was a good kisser—"good" as in he had the power to make her forget some pretty important things, like what time it was, her first name, and what planet she was on.

"Is this okay?" Paul asked softly as he pulled her closer.

"Mmm, yes, that feels great," she murmured.

Just then Cordelia managed to wiggle so the stone shifted out from underneath her without Paul noticing a thing. What a relief. She could finally enjoy the Paul Morgan lip-lock experience.

Yeah, not a chance. Cordelia could never turn her brain off, even if someone paid her a million dollars to throw the switch. While she was thinking about how Paul's breath was so sweet and his lips were so soft, she was simultaneously obsessing that her own breath might smell like feet, the really sweaty kind. She hadn't been able to brush her teeth since last night. She also reminded herself that she usually slept with her mouth open, so who knew what might have flown in there!

Paul stopped nuzzling her neck for a minute to look deep into her eyes. He never let a day go by without mentioning how remarkably blue hers were, but she didn't expect him to say anything nice about the icky white stuff that was surely stuck in the corners of them now. He ran his hands through her long honey-blond hair, which Cordelia assumed felt greasy and disgusting—she hadn't had a chance to wash out the styling product build-up.

Why, oh why didn't I wake up at the crack of dawn to take a shower? Cordelia thought. Then she remembered the questionable conditions of public campground rest-rooms and the answer became crystal clear.

She tried to distract herself by slipping a hand under Paul's T-shirt and tracing the shape of a heart on his back with her fingertip. For a non-jock, he had the most amazingly buff swimmer-type body. Ripped abs, arms that were toned (not jacked), broad shoulders. Cordelia had to restrain herself from climbing all over him as if he were a rock wall. Speaking of which, Paul was slightly over six feet tall and towered over Cordelia's small, five-foot-three frame. Even lying down next to him, she felt dwarfed, but that was fine with her. It almost made her feel protected.

Protection seemed to be on Paul's mind, too. As they were pressed up against each other tightly, he stretched out over Cordelia and made a move for his wallet. She knew what was in there. They had talked about this before. He'd only been with one person, which is very respectable for a seventeen-year-old guy. And noble too. As for Cordelia, she had just turned sixteen a couple of weeks ago and had racked up a big whopping zero con-quests overall. She was cool with it, though. She was just waiting for the right person, and the right time and place.

Paul leaned back over her and delicately kissed her forehead. "You take my breath away, you know that?" he whispered.

All right, it seems like I have the right guy, chirped the voice inside Cordelia's head. After all, they had been going out for a few months and he was super-hot and incredibly nice.

But was this the right time and place? Highly doubtful. If it happened here and now, it would be an impromptu, spontaneous event, and those never happened to Cordelia Packer, the most structured, organized, type-A teenage girl in San Diego. In fact, Cordelia was the reason the Container Store existed and why Excel spreadsheets had been invented. Even if Cordelia *had* planned on Paul going into his wallet to dig out something that had a wrapper (but wasn't a piece of gum), she hadn't planned on being this nervous and sick to her stomach. She didn't feel right. A vision of Alexis Dunbar and the word *F-O-R-S-Y-T-H-I-A* flashed before her eyes. This was definitely not good. She had to do something quick, or else Paul would be covered in last night's veggie burgers.

"I think I need to go to the bathroom," she said abruptly.

Not really all that classy, but hey, when you gotta go, you gotta go.

"Now?" Paul asked.

Cordelia could tell he was disappointed. "I know, bad timing."

"That's okay." Paul closed his wallet and tossed it to

the other side of the tent. "You have to listen when nature calls, right?"

"Yeah, sorry about that," Cordelia said while giving his right hand an affectionate squeeze.

"Don't be sorry. We'll pick up where we left off some other time," Paul said with a smile.

The guy couldn't be any more perfect. Another boy might have argued with her. Or begged, whined, and complained. But Paul was so much more mature and sensitive and understanding. Sometimes he seemed older than his seventeen years. Maybe that was why her parents were so impressed with him. She couldn't imagine them letting her go off camping with just any Joe Schmo. Yet there was something about Paul that made you trust him.

Maybe it was his gentleness or his humility or the way his shaggy brown hair always looked so disheveled. There was nothing manic or hyper about Paul either—no macho posturing, no posing or phoniness. He was honest and as natural as the Tom's of Maine personal hygiene products he used. He seemed to be everything Cordelia had ever wanted.

So why the hell did I freak out just now? Cordelia thought as she made her way out of the tent.

"Hey, could you grab a paper cup or something from the ladies' room? I just spotted a lizard in here and I want to find a good spot for it in the woods," Paul called out.

Cordelia shivered. Lizard? *In the tent?* She had no idea how Paul could be so "one with the outdoors." The stuff that Paul liked to do—camping, hiking, bird-watching—all could be filed under the category *Anti-Cordelia*. She mostly preferred the indoors, where she could make the environment suit her. Temperature in her bedroom too hot? Turn up the air. Too dark to read in the living room? Turn on a light. And there were doors and locks to keep out any unwanted intruders or scaly, slimy living creatures. Here in the wilderness, she had absolutely no control. As far as Cordelia was concerned, it was just plain anarchy. The only exception to the "Outside Bad, Inside Good" rule was, of course, the beach.

Cordelia trudged over to the public restroom, stepping on twigs and leaves along the way. In the distance, she could have sworn she heard the roll of the surf and smelled the saltiness of the Pacific air. Maybe before heading home she and Paul could go take a nice stroll along the shoreline and get their feet wet. It wasn't on the itinerary that he had drawn up before the trip (which she'd encouraged him to do, of course), but neither was the lizard. Unfortunately, surprises happen. And even though they wouldn't be looking through binoculars at some rare natural specimen, it would be fun, right?

Certainly Paul could see that she was going out of her way to participate in the things that mattered to him. She'd already given up junk food (including Taco

Bell—her passion!) because he was worried about her LDL levels or pesticides on the shredded lettuce or something like that. She was currently in a public camp-ground bathroom, touching a bunch of grimy sink fix-tures without the hope of having any anti-bacterial soap come out of the dispensers. And in a few minutes, she was apparently going to help him start a lizard reloca-tion program. Surely he could stop at the beach for a few minutes and appease her tiny, insignificant wishes, right?

Of course, he can. Cordelia decided to mention it to him the moment after they scooped up that lizard with a Dixie cup.

Or maybe she could say something even sooner. When she came out of the bathroom, Paul was standing right in front of her, all aglow in the morning sunlight.

"Whoa, where did you come from?" Cordelia said, startled. Then she thought about their tent being occu-pied by a lizard. "Did you leave that...thing... alone...with our stuff?"

"Oh, I just picked up the little guy up with my hands and put him down on a mossy log. No biggie," Paul replied nonchalantly.

"With your hands?" Cordelia swore she heard *for-sythia* spelling itself out again in her head.

"I'm scrubbed-in like a surgeon, so don't worry." Paul laughed.

"Hey, no fair. I had to touch everything in there with my knees."

Paul laughed even harder. "Cordy, you've got to relax. I don't think you've taken one deep, cleansing breath since we've gotten here."

Cordelia shrugged. Paul was very into meditating, so much so that he could probably have given Buddhist monks a run for their money. She had thought about giving in to Paul's gentle suggestions and trying meditation herself, but even if she did, she seriously doubted that she could ever reach his level of tranquillity. She was too busy evaluating everything she did, planning what she would do next, and consulting her to-do lists, that there never seemed to be a good enough time to inhale, exhale, and let all of it go.

Suddenly, Paul's eyes widened as he peered over Cordelia's shoulder. "You're not going to believe this," he said, "but I think I heard a red-legged honeycreeper."

"Cool," she replied.

He smiled. "You don't know what I'm talking about, do you?"

"Well, I'm assuming it's some kind of a bird."

"It's pretty rare to find that species around here." Paul glanced at his digital watch. "Damn, we're going to have to check out soon. Want to get some quick birding in before we leave?"

Cordelia wanted to be honest. She'd already made

up the having-to-pee story in order to get out of going too far with Paul. Now, here she was in a similar situation. She wanted to go to the beach instead of scour the forest in search of wildlife. She knew she should just say something and that he'd be fine with it. But Cordelia felt a little guilty for depriving him once already today, and if she denied him the red honey something-or-other, that just might be too much for him to take.

"Go get your binoculars," Cordelia said, and kissed him on the cheek.

Paul appeared to be overjoyed. "You're the best," he said, hugging her. "Be right back."

Cordelia put her wistful thoughts of frothy, warm saltwater and a gentle tepid breeze out of her mind, and tried to remind herself that although she'd never had a reason to compromise before, she had a good one now.

*   *   *

Cordelia and Paul hiked for about a half hour, but they never found the red-legged whatever. Paul seemed a little disappointed, even though he'd kept telling her that they weren't really common to Southern California. Cordelia hadn't minded at all, though. Some of Paul's words had been repeating themselves in her brain—"Maybe someday we'll go birding in Colorado. That's where you can see some special ones."

I can't wait, Cordelia thought as Paul's gold Toyota Prius hybrid zipped down Route 75. The sun was out in full force, and she could feel her skin soaking up large quantities of vitamin D. Paul had insisted that they roll down the windows and cool off the un-artificial way, but Cordelia somehow convinced him to put on the air-conditioning instead. Humidity always dehydrated her and did funky things to her hair. Besides, she had just tamed it with a cute ponytail and didn't want fifty-five-mile-per-hour winds to mess it up.

This explanation made Paul chuckle—apparently he found Cordelia's little quirks very entertaining. He put an arm around her shoulder. "It's such a beautiful day. I hope it's like this the entire summer."

Cordelia tried to swallow the lump that had formed in her throat. She'd known this day was coming. Paul had informed her about his plans when they first met at the Twelfth Annual Mission Bay High School Quiz Tournament. Her team had kicked his team's butt and afterward Paul had come by to congratulate her on the big win. Cordelia had been so nervous talking to him, especially because Alexis Dunbar was in the vicinity. Luckily, Paul had been so easygoing that Cordelia's anxiety had disappeared within minutes. A few days later, they went to this club called Hot Monkey Love Café and talked for hours. They chatted about how summer loomed in the distance, and that's when he dropped the bomb. From late June until early August, he'd be giving tours at Yosemite National Park, more than four hundred miles away.

It had seemed so far off in the distance back then, but now the moment was here. Even though Paul was going to be out of sight, Cordelia knew that he'd never be out of her mind. She gazed out the window and tried not to get all blubbery in front of him. She definitely didn't want his last memories of her to involve watery red eyes and snot.

Paul moved his hand down to her leg and began to rub it gently. "Hey, I'm going to miss you."

Cordelia took her gaze off the trees whizzing by and looked at him. She put both her flip-flop-adorned feet onto the dashboard. Paul raised his eyebrows a little bit, so she thought better of it and put them back on the floor.

"What have you been thinking about?" Paul asked. "You've been quiet for most of the trip."

"How much I'm going to miss you," she replied, then bit her lip. Maybe she shouldn't have said that. Her older sister, Molly, who was pretty much a legend at Mission Bay High, had only written one list in her lifetime. It was called Molly Packer's Rules to Getting Any Guy You Want, and rule number seven was: "Never let a boy know you're crazy about him. He'll lose interest, and then you'll be a loser."

Cordelia tried to banish her sister's words to a far-away, desertlike region of her mind. Clearly, Molly didn't know what she was talking about, because right now Paul was looking at her with more than interest in his eyes. She felt pretty damn sure he was just as crazy about her.

"Well, I'm sure you're going to have plenty of distractions," Paul said, grinning.

"Oh, whatever. My head will be in the books."

"Yeah, right," Paul said mockingly. "You and your sister are going to be spending the entire summer in Eureka, a total college town, without your parents. That apartment is going to be party central."

"Molly will be partying," she said. "I will be studying. C'mon, you know me well enough to know that when college credit courses become available at a cheap state school like Molly's, I'm the first one in line to sign up."

"Stop it," Paul said. "You're turning me on."

Cordelia let out a big laugh. Paul rarely made jokes like that. *It must be the sun beating through the windshield.* Cordelia reached into her backpack, which was on the floor beneath her. She tried to ignore that she had three days' worth of stubble to hack into later and focused on what she was looking for. Her prized possession— her Treo. The thing was made for multitaskers and organizing addicts like Cordelia. With this gadget, she could e-mail Paul directions to Yosemite, call her mom and tell her to order a pizza—no, wait, a nice garden salad—for dinner, and access all her important documents, lists, and other items that proved she was one of the most anal-retentive people on Earth.

She was about to go on the Internet and Google "symptoms of sunstroke" when the Treo started to buzz. She had a voice mail message. Cordelia glanced over at Paul, who seemed to be staring down the road and acting normal, so she thought it was safe to listen to it. What she heard was the familiar, deliriously upbeat voice of Molly Packer.

"Hey, it's me! I'm so happy you're coming! Do me a favor. Look in my closet at home for my jean skirt. Not the long James skirt, the Joie. It's a mini with a pleat in the front. Could you bring it when you come? Oh, and my yellow slingbacks, the ones from Marc Jacobs, bring those too. No, wait a minute, never mind, I just found them under my bed. It's the pink Jimmy Choos I need. And would you look in my dresser and see if you can find my white Juicy halter top? And anything else you can find that's really summer sexy. You won't believe this complex where we'll be living. It's a serious scene, especially around the pool. And there's a clubhouse where—"

Cordelia didn't need to hear any more. She cut off the message and tossed the Treo back into her JanSport.

Paul gave Cordelia a curious look. "What's wrong? Bad news?"

She rolled her eyes. "Oh, no, just a message from my sister," she grumbled. "She has me on high fashion alert."

He chuckled a bit, and then got all serious. "If you just close your eyes and breathe in through your nose and out through your mouth, the stress will just melt away."

Easy for him to say, Cordelia thought. Sometimes when Paul said stuff like that, it sounded a little condescending. But she just tried to shake it off and change the subject.

"I'm almost prepared for my poli-sci class," she said enthusiastically. Cordelia had known she wanted to be a lawyer ever since her gigantic crush on Dylan McDermott on *The Practice*.

Paul smirked. "More prepared than they are to butt heads with the debate team captain."

"Co-captain," Cordelia corrected. She shared the title with Alexis Dunbar, of course.

"I bet Molly is excited to have you there."

Cordelia shrugged. "I guess."

Paul pulled a packet of Listerine breath strips out of his cargo shorts pocket and placed one on his tongue. Chills proceeded to ravage Cordelia's body. "I get the feeling you're not too thrilled with the idea of spending two months with your sister," he said.

Cordelia wondered if it was too soon in their relationship to bring up family problems. She wasn't even sure whether or not Molly constituted a "problem." Molly was just…Molly.

"We're very different," she said finally. "Molly's more…" She tried to think of the right expression, something that wouldn't make her sound like a jerk. "Well, she's a little flaky."

Paul took his eyes off the road just long enough to give her a look of total disbelief. "*You* have a sister who's flaky?"

She wasn't surprised by his reaction. People always had a hard time believing they were sisters. Actually, there were times when Cordelia was absolutely certain that some mix-up happened at the hospital nursery and that she really belonged to Monica Geller from *Friends*. "Molly kind of lives for the moment, and she doesn't think about the consequences of her actions. Not that she's a bad person," Cordelia added hastily. "She's really sweet and generous. But sometimes…well, she can be, I dunno, clueless."

"Then it's good she'll have you to look after her this summer," Paul said.

Cordelia frowned. "Oh, joy of joys."

"Hey, maybe this will get your spirits up. I burned you a CD to take with you to Eureka."

Oh my God, how incredibly sweet! Cordelia thought.

"It's in the glove compartment. Go ahead and put it on."

A moment later, the sound of rain falling, birds

cooing, and leaves rustling filled the car. *Okay, it's not the Black Eyed Peas, but that's cool.*

"This is great, thanks." Cordelia leaned over and kissed Paul on the cheek. He put his arm around her waist and pulled her close for a soft yet quick peck on the lips. Then she sat back in her seat, closed her eyes, and tried to appreciate the "music." But instead of tuning out, her thoughts went back to Molly.

Cordelia could see her sister now, lying on the roof of her building, lathered in baby oil, getting a tan. Molly really was striking, with her light blond hair, green eyes, and a body that would make Halle Berry give up being hot. While Molly had always been a boy magnet and popular, Cordelia had found herself in the bookworm, activities-geek role, which is why she thought being with Paul was the biggest stroke of luck in her life. Paul looked like the kind of guy Molly would go after, and here he was, holding Cordelia's hand.

It was just like her mom had predicted a few years ago. She used to say, "There will be boyfriends and dates and good times for you, too, Cordy. You'll catch up."

But then Cordelia had usually responded pretty negatively. One of her favorite comebacks to comments like that had been, "I don't want to catch up. I don't want to be like Molly."

In fact, sometimes Cordelia thought that her need for structure and planning and organization was all in reaction to Molly's fly-by-the-seat-of-her-Urban-Outfitters-panties persona. And to this day, Molly still tried to snap her out of it and get Cordelia to let her guard down. Cordelia wondered, *Why do I put up so much of a fight?*

Paul's voice broke into her reverie. "Wasn't that amazing?"

"What?" Then she realized he had to be talking about the Sounds of Nature CD she hadn't been listening to. "Oh, right, yes, it was fantastic."

"Awesome, you can play it on the flight to Eureka."

Suddenly, Cordelia's palms began to sweat. *You're not even on a plane right now, dork. Calm down!* she told herself.

"You okay?" Paul asked when he noticed how pale she had gotten.

Cordelia hated confessing this irrational fear of hers, but she couldn't see any way of getting out of it. She was practically hyperventilating right now and they were only *talking* about flying. "Don't laugh, but I'm afraid of planes. Well, not planes, really. Flying. Actually, not flying. It's more a fear of crashing. Crashing and dying."

Paul tried to swallow a laugh. "That's okay. Lots of people hate flying."

"Yeah, I know. It's a drag. Trust me, I'd rather not spend a million hours on a bus."

Cordelia looked around and immediately recognized the San Diego streets. The reality of their imminent separation hit her, and she felt terrible. Gorge-yourself-on-Taco-Bell terrible. But she wouldn't give in to temptation. No, she would stay strong for the greater good of this relationship, or at least until Paul left and he couldn't catch her sneaking one little, tiny gordita....

"You know I'd really love it if you'd come and visit me for a weekend. How about it?"

Cordelia was psyched. "Absolutely! And maybe you could come to Eureka?"

"Sure. Let me find out what kind of schedule I'll have."

She smiled and gazed out the window again, feeling giddy that Paul had suggested that they make *plans* to see each other! They were cruising alongside the coast now, and between houses she caught glimpses of the beach. She couldn't help but feel just a little mournful about not asking him to stop there earlier today. Maybe they could have lain out on the sand and baked under the sun until they couldn't bear the heat one minute more. Then they might have raced into the water, jumped into a wave, the sensation of cold water hitting their hot skin. She would have absolutely loved that. Oh, and her boyfriend would have been shirtless....

Paul's strained voice caught her attention. "I can't believe those people."

"Huh?"

"On the beach, just lying there. Don't they have any

idea what the sun is doing to their health? I mean, we've put this enormous hole in the ozone and now everyone's, like, mindlessly singeing their skin cells, waiting to get cancer. I bet these guys are the ones causing all the smog and pollution to begin with."

Well, that's pretty extreme, Cordelia thought. There were such things as sunscreen and umbrellas to create shade. And was it necessary for Paul to get so perturbed about total strangers, who were doing nothing but sunbathing?

"Sorry, it's just the public unawareness that bothers me. I didn't mean to go off like that. You must think I'm really weird," Paul said nervously.

She put her hand on Paul's knee and gave it a tender squeeze. "That's okay. I'm weird too."

And he only knows the half of it.

Chapter Two

Cordelia stood at the front door of her rambling white ranch house and stared at the steps where she and Paul had said good-bye. They had this silly tradition that always made her giggle. She'd stand on the top of the stairs and Paul would stand at the bottom so they could be around the same height when they hugged and kissed. A few minutes ago, Paul had his hands on her tiny waist, and Cordelia could feel him breathing heavily when his mouth was on hers.

When he drove away, she felt an instantaneous aching in her stomach, which she assumed was caused by Paul's departure. But now that she'd been standing there for a while thinking about it, she realized that she was still bothered by what she'd done earlier that morning.

Why had she run out on such a big moment with Paul? If things between them were so perfect—just the way she had dreamed they would be—then something had to be the matter with her.

"Cordy, is that you?" Her mother's voice floated out from the back of the house. "Honey, I need your help in the kitchen."

Cordelia dragged her backpack behind her through the foyer and then the den, which her parents had redecorated right before her birthday. Her mom liked every room in the house to have a theme—the master bedroom was called "Jungle" because it was covered in animal prints, and the guest bathroom was called "Sunlight" because everything in it was the same shade of yellow. Her mom and dad never went into Molly's space, and why would they? It was dubbed "The VIP Room," after all.

As for Cordelia's bedroom, it had the most unspectacular theme ever. Her father called it "The Library" because he couldn't build enough shelves for all the books on Cordelia's summer reading list. She had to resort to using her Elfa closet organizing system to hold both her clothes and her prized first edition *Chronicles of Narnia* collection. Molly had nearly cried when Cordelia got rid of a stack of old jeans in order to make room for classic children's literature.

When Cordelia finally appeared in the kitchen, her mother was unloading groceries from several large paper bags that were placed neatly on the counter. This room was named "Spice," so the palette here consisted of earth tones. There were lots of dried flowers and herbs accenting tabletops and walls. Scented candles sat on the windowsill near the sink, and baskets of fresh California fruit were scattered around to make the room feel warm and welcoming. But Cordelia's favorite part of the kitchen was, strangely, the inside of the cabinets. Mrs. Packer had compartmentalized and organized every drawer and shelf, labeled a place for every jar and can, and separated the different kinds of utensils into categories like "daily use" and "infrequent use."

It was no mystery who Cordelia got her type-A gene from.

"Could you put away all the perishables while I unload the rest?" her mom asked.

Cordelia took a carton of orange juice from her and stuck it in the refrigerator. Then she grabbed the eggs and 2 percent milk as her mother stacked up cans of tomato paste and jars of dill pickles, her father's favorite. She and her mom got into a natural rhythm with the unpacking, each of them knowing exactly where all the items went. Cordelia quickly glanced at her mom as she stretched on her tiptoes to reach a cabinet that was too high up. The only physical resemblance she shared with her mother was their height, or lack of it. Everything else was pure Molly—the eyes, the hair, and the smile. If her mom ever decided to invest in some stilts, she'd be the spitting image of her older, VIP daughter.

"You won't believe who I ran into at the farmers market," her mom said excitedly.

Cordelia rolled her eyes. Her mom had a tendency to create drama when none was necessary, just like someone else she knew.

"I don't know. Who?"

Her mom scrubbed her hands furiously in the sink. "Guess."

Cordelia's mind ran over relatives who hadn't been around lately. "Aunt Ella."

"No."

"Governor Arnold Schwarzenegger. He called you a girly-man!"

Her mom laughed and snapped a hand towel at Cordelia's rear end. "No, smart mouth."

"Well, just tell me, then!"

Her mother beamed. "Jake!"

"Jake," Cordelia repeated. "Jake who?"

"Jacob Stein. Remember? Molly's old boyfriend."

Normally, at this point, Cordelia would still be clueless. Molly had so many boyfriends, she'd never been able to keep them straight. Unfortunately, Cordelia remembered Jacob Stein as much as she wished she could forget him.

"Maybe you should wash your hands again."

"Oh, Cordy, stop it," her mother chided her. "He's a nice boy. And he adores Molly."

"They *all* adore Molly," Cordelia said. She took a sack of peaches from the bag and began arranging them in another wicker basket.

"Yes, well, your father and I always liked him. Maybe it was because he never acted like we were parents, you know? He actually talked to us."

Yeah, he'd talk to anyone who would listen to him. He never shut up; that was the problem, she thought.

"And even though he could have showered more often, he had lovely manners," her mother continued.

Cordelia shook her head wearily. Her mom had definitely passed down her naïve streak to Molly. Neither of them realized that Jacob Stein was the king of kissing ass. He was always laying it on thick and trying to score points with Molly and her folks. Cordelia couldn't believe that she was the only person who really saw through his act—and he knew it, which is why they had fought like crazy when no one else was around.

"Manners? Mom, did you *not* eat dinner with him every night for five months? The guy wiped his mouth on his sleeve. His sleeve!"

"You're exaggerating. He only did that once."

Cordelia crossed her arms and gave her mother a hard stare.

"Okay, maybe more than once," her mom reconsidered. "Anyway, Jake and I had a nice long talk at the market."

"About Molly, I suppose."

"Well, of course, he asked about her. But he asked about you, too."

"I'm so thrilled."

Her mother ignored the sarcasm. "I asked him about school. He told me that he went to UNLV last year, but he's not going back."

Now, *that* was interesting. Jake had been such a know-it-all, and talked as if he was an authority on every subject, but Cordelia had a strong feeling he was just full of it. Maybe he flunked out or something.

"Well, what happened?"

"He didn't get into that. He just said he didn't like the atmosphere."

Well, that makes sense, too, Cordelia thought. Jake had struck her as the kind of person who had trouble committing to a goal. He was always bragging about his plans to form some sort of revolutionary alt-rock band with his friends, or hitchhike across the country with only the clothes on his back. But each time Cordelia asked him about his progress, there never seemed to be any.

"And he said there wasn't a good music scene in Las Vegas."

Cordelia rolled her eyes. She remembered that Jake

had been a pseudo-intellectual snob about music. He only liked obscure indie bands that no one else had ever heard of, and if any of them became successful, he'd bash them for "selling out."

Actually, he had an opinion about *everything*, and it drove Cordelia up a wall.

"He wants to transfer to a college in Seattle," her mother added.

Cordelia took the last avocado from the bag and put it on the windowsill to ripen. "That's great, Mom. I'm going to take a shower."

"Hang on, I haven't told you the big news yet. In another minute, you're going to thank me."

"For what?"

"I told Jake that you're going up to Eureka to spend the summer with Molly. And how's this for a coincidence? *He's* thinking of driving up north to look at that college in Seattle!"

Cordelia was suddenly aware of that familiar churning sensation in her stomach. She was afraid to ask the next question.

"And...what does that have to do with me?"

"He offered to give you a ride!"

Cordelia did everything in her power not to grab her mother and shake some sense into her. "*What?*"

"He said the timing is perfect, and it would be right on his way. Isn't that nice?"

"*Nice?*" she shrieked. "Mom, I don't want to be stuck in a car with Jake Stein all the way to Eureka!"

"So you'd rather spend the time on a bus?" Her mother pursed her lips. "With total strangers."

Okay, that's one point for Mom, she thought. Her mother was right—traveling with Jake couldn't possibly be as bad as being stuck on a dirty old bus with a crying baby or a mentally unstable person with a bad case of B.O. Her parents wanted to give Cordelia a ride, but their work schedules were incredibly tight. Her father was working on an important ad campaign for Burt's Bees and her mom was organizing a gala event for the Red Cross. They just couldn't get any time off now.

"No, it's just that…how do we know Jake isn't a speed demon, or has a bad case of narcolepsy that might interfere with his driving?"

Mrs. Packer chuckled. "Narcolepsy?"

"Too much?"

"Listen, if you don't want to go with Jake, that's entirely up to you. I think it's a terrific idea, though. You guys can go at your own pace and pull over and see some sights. And since you can't share in the driving, I told him we'd pay for the gas. So it works out for everyone."

Cordelia sighed in near defeat. "Fine, I'll think about it."

"Good," her mother said, smiling. "So are you going to tell me about the big camping trip?"

Cordelia cringed a little bit. The thought of telling her mom the details of her tent romps with Paul made her feel light-headed. "It was great." She tried to come up with something else that might satisfy her mother's curiosity without raising any I-need-to-have-an-embarrassing-sex-talk-with-my-daughter red flags. "We saw some birds."

Oh God, that's going to make her think of "bees"! I'm done for, she thought.

"Wow, that's neat. Paul does love that nature stuff," her mom replied. "I'm glad you had fun."

All of a sudden, Cordelia was annoyed. She just spent days in a forest with a guy who resembled that latest Abercrombie & Fitch catalog cover model! That was the only thing her mom was going to say? Wasn't she concerned? Didn't she care?

But then Cordelia thought about what would have happened if this had been Molly. Her parents wouldn't have even let her sister go on a trip with her boyfriend to begin with. In fact, they had a lot of rules when it came to Molly. She remembered how her mom had explained it a while back—Molly was a free spirit and needed a little more guidance. As for Cordelia, her parents used to joke that she was the most responsible child, even when she was in the womb. So it made perfect sense that Cordelia was expected to do the right thing, follow the smarter path, avoid risk, and make sensible decisions.

And it was the reason why Mrs. Packer probably didn't think it was necessary to press Cordelia any further about her weekend.

"Well, lunch will be ready soon," her mom said as she got out the ingredients for her famous chicken salad. "Want to take that shower now?"

Cordelia ran her fingers through her hair, which felt as if it had been covered in Crisco. A shower was exactly what she needed to stop her mind from buzzing about Molly, her mom, Jacob Stein, Paul, and everything else that was bothering her.

*   *   *

Several minutes later, Cordelia scrubbed herself furiously with Origins Pomegranate Wash. Not only was her mind still buzzing, but now she was pretty much consumed with thoughts of Jake Stein. No way, *no way* was she going to spend all that time in a car with him. One of them would surely end up in a body bag. Cordelia also suspected that Jake had ulterior motives behind this favor. He was probably doing it just to see Molly again. *Wait, maybe it's even more than that. Maybe he wants to get back together with her!*

Cordelia rubbed some mint conditioning rinse onto her scalp. If that were true, then her whole family could be doomed. For some unknown reason, Molly had this

big soft spot for Jake—she hadn't stayed friends with any
of her exes, except for him. They had lost touch during
college, but Molly and Jake had spent a lot of time
together at school during senior year, to the point where
everyone thought they were still going out. What if Jake
professed his undying love for Molly and they got mar-
ried and moved back into her parents' place together and
ruined every single waking moment of Cordelia's life?

She inhaled the fresh scent of her shaving cream and
tried to calm down. She was letting her imagination get
the best of her. Molly was definitely over Jake. She was
seeing a new guy every three weeks and living it up as
usual. Actually, now that Cordelia thought about it,
what had Molly seen in Jake in the first place? Molly
used to claim that he was funnier than Dave Chappelle,
but Cordelia had never seen any evidence of that. She
just thought he was extremely obnoxious. Cordelia's
mind flashed back to a year ago. Jake had been over for
dinner—*again*—and he'd told everyone about some
friend of his who had been suspended for cheating.

"It was an essay test, for History of Visual
Aesthetics," Jake had reported. "One question: 'Discuss
the impact of Leonardo da Vinci on Western art.' We
had an hour and a half to write and the teacher gave
everyone two blue books to write in."

"How could anyone cheat on that kind of test?" Mr.
Packer had wanted to know.

"Greg wrote one sentence. 'And so it is clear that Leonardo da Vinci had a great impact on Western art.' Then he wrote '#2' on the cover of the blue book. He really believed the teacher would think she'd lost the first one. Personally, I think he should get credit for his creativity."

Her parents had laughed, and Molly had practically fallen out of her chair in hysterics. But Cordelia had only been able to choke on her pork chop. Of course, Jake had been sitting next to her and seen she was struggling, so he slapped her hard on the back, which only made things worse.

Jake Stein. She could see him now, but just barely. He was very nondescript and very blah looking. He was short for a guy—not more than five foot seven. He had shoulder-length hair and was a tad on the scrawny side. Not only did he have a crummy personality, he wasn't even that cute. Molly must have been going through some emotional or self-esteem crisis to consider dating him.

After her shower, Cordelia sat down at her desk and considered the situation with a clearer, cleaner body, mind, and soul. She knew her parents wouldn't force her to accept Jake's offer of a ride, but she figured they'd feel a lot better if she were traveling with someone they trusted, however misguided their presumptions about Jake might be. She knew her mother was already feeling guilty that she couldn't drive Cordelia up herself. *Hmm*.

Sitting on a Greyhound bus for twenty and a half hours with two transfers—how grubby would *that* make her feel? No chance to wash up or change into fresh clothes. Using gas station restrooms, eating sandwiches that came out of machines. None of this was good at all.

Wait a minute, Cordelia said to herself. *Maybe I don't have to be on the road for that many hours straight with Jake.* She could break the trip up over several days. They could spend the nights in separate rooms at nice, respectable motels so that they could have downtime, which might prevent them from killing each other. If she turned up the tunes on her iPod, she wouldn't have to make much conversation with Jake in the car.

This line of thought was making the situation seem a little more acceptable. She went to her desk and sat down in front of her PowerBook. She brought up the Google search she had downloaded from her Treo and clicked on the link for a map of the West Coast.

A wide smile crept across Cordelia's face. She knew that Yosemite National Park was somewhere between San Diego and Eureka, but she hadn't realized it was almost exactly the same distance from each of the two cities. It wasn't in a direct line—actually, it was way off to the east, closer to the Nevada border than the Pacific coast. But so what? She could see Paul! And if her parents were paying for the gas, Jake would just have to deal with going the way *she* wanted to go.

Feeling a hundred times better, she went onto MapQuest and began researching. First, she checked the direct distance from San Diego to Eureka. According to the figures that popped up on the screen, it was 766 miles and approximately twelve hours' driving time. She did a quick calculation. Allowing stops for meals and breaks, she decided it would be more like fifteen hours, maybe more. Then she cleared the fields and put Yosemite into the plan.

A click brought her eyes to the upper right-hand corner of the screen. There was an instant message from PedroLion.

PedroLion? She didn't recognize the screen name. There was a Pedro in her history class, though she couldn't imagine why he'd be sending her an instant message. Did he have a question about the Magna Carta or something?

PedroLion: Eureka! Road trip!

Her eyes narrowed. It could be only one person.

CPacker515: Jake?
PedroLion: Hey, Cordy! What's up?

Cordelia swallowed hard. *And so it begins....*

CPacker515: I'm on MapQuest, figuring out what to do about my trip.

PedroLion: Doesn't surprise me. Are you going to compare MapQuest info with Yahoo! Maps, just to make sure you're getting the most precise route?

She had only been chatting with him for mere seconds, and he was already infuriating. *How dare he accuse me of being so nitpicky? He's right, but still!*

CPacker515: Puh-lease. I don't need to double-check that stuff.

PedroLion: Yeah, right. You need to TRIPLE-check it.

CPacker515: Well, if I'm going to be traveling with you, Magellan, maybe I should.

Ha! Got you there! Cordelia thought as she pounded on the keyboard.

PedroLion: What do you mean "if"? You have better prospects?

CPacker515: If you keep it up, I'll WALK.

PedroLion: Okay, okay. Seriously, it'll be fun. And I could use the company.

I'll bet, Cordelia thought. *It's a wonder this guy has any friends at all.*

CPacker515: Well, I did some light research, and I thought we could break up the trip like so.
PedroLion: Oh God.
CPacker515: Relax, it's not that bad.
CPacker515: What do you think of this? Day 1: San Diego to Yosemite, 430 miles, 7 hours driving. Day 2: Yosemite. Day 3: Yosemite to Eureka, 484 miles, 8 1/2 hours driving.
PedroLion: Wait, why are we going to Yosemite?

Cordelia could feel her blood pressure rising.

CPacker515: I want to stop there and see my boyfriend, Paul.
PedroLion: Hahahahahahaha
CPacker515: What's so funny?!?!
PedroLion: Nothing.

Now she wanted to reach through her screen and strangle him.

PedroLion: Let's play it by ear. Peace out.

Then he signed off, leaving Cordelia to cover her ears as she let out a loud, earth-shattering groan.

*   *   *

Over the next hour, nothing else existed in Cordelia's world but hotel websites, reservation forms, tourism board lists, and expense spreadsheets. She was in full OCD mode and determined to turn the stench of this crappy situation into the sweet smell of success. Her mom was so thrilled that she was going to take Jake up on his offer, she gave Cordelia her credit card and told her to book whatever rooms she wanted. This definitely made her mood brighter. Cordelia also worked up a neat itinerary that involved some good beach pit stops in San Luis Obispo and a few other beautiful areas. This would really help her to unwind and keep her mind focused on positive stuff, like her visit with Paul, the class she was going to take in late July, and hell, even getting a chance to hang out with Molly. Everything was starting to look up.

Speaking of which, Cordelia remembered that she hadn't listened to the rest of her sister's voice mail message. Not that she had originally intended to, but hey, maybe Molly was going to say something important like, make sure to bring a deadbolt for your room because I live in a really sketchy part of town and homeless people pace in front of my building all night. But before she could retrieve the message, her Treo vibrated on her desk. She glanced at the caller ID, which read: *Molly's 3rd cell.*

"Hello?"

Before Molly even spoke, Cordelia could hear her and some other girl laughing. "Hi, Cordy. It's me."

"You sound…busy."

"No, we're just…never mind. Did you get my message earlier?"

Cordelia recited from memory: "Miniskirt, pink Jimmy Choos, white halter top."

"You rock, little sis. What are you going to bring? Oh, wait, I got it. That purple spaghetti strap dress I gave you for your birthday. That'll totally show off your legs."

"But I hardly have any legs. I'm short," she replied.

"So is the dress. That's the point. To make your legs look longer," Molly said through the other girl's chatter.

"I haven't even thought about it yet."

"Well, start thinking," Molly said sharply. "We'll be going out a lot."

"Molly, I'm taking a course in political science. I'll have to study."

"I know, I know. But you need to have some fun, too, right? Hold on, Cordelia. You're not going to be boring, are you?"

"What's *that* supposed to mean?"

"Oh, don't be so touchy," Molly declared. "I just want us to have some good times this summer, okay? I miss you."

Cordelia was taken aback. Was this true? Molly hadn't said that since she arrived at college, and even then, Cordelia thought that was just the separation anxiety talking.

"Really?"

"Uh, of course! How many sisters do I have?"

"Not counting the sorority ones?" Cordelia joked.

Molly's voice wilted a little. "Ha-ha. I can't wait to hear all these hilarious lines of yours in person."

"I'm only kidding. Hey, I promise to equally balance my studying and partying. Sound good?"

"Sounds perfect," Molly said sweetly. "I could read some stuff, too, you know. Get a head start on next semester, like you always do."

Cordelia smiled. "Great!"

Maybe this won't be as bad as I thought. Maybe Molly is finally getting her act together.

"Oh shit." Molly gasped.

"What?"

"Is today the sixteenth?"

"Yeah, why?"

"I was supposed to give the landlord my deposit before the fifteenth."

Then again, maybe not.

"Well, you'd better do it now, before you get evicted," Cordelia advised.

"Right, right. I will." She could hear Molly rummaging around, most likely looking for her misplaced checkbook or a lost pen. "So when are you coming up?"

Cordelia raised an eyebrow. She was very curious about how her sister was going to react to her news. "First, let me tell you *how* I'm coming up. You're not going to believe this. Jacob Stein is giving me a ride."

She had to hold the phone away from her ear while Molly shrieked.

"You're kidding! Jake's coming *here*?"

Cordelia had a bad feeling about this.

"Uh, yeah. Mom ran into him and mentioned that I was going to spend the summer with you. He's going to Seattle to visit some school and he offered to drop me on his way. I don't know if he's really going to Seattle or not. He might just be doing this as an excuse to see you."

Molly was still causing a ruckus on her end of the line. "Really? You think so?"

"Maybe. You never know with that guy." Cordelia paused for a second while her sister let out a series of giggles. "Molly, you sound like you *want* to see him."

"Well, I wouldn't mind. He's such a sweetie!"

"A what-ie?"

Molly laughed. "I know you guys didn't hit it off, but he's really one of the nicest boys I ever dated."

This was *not* what Cordelia had expected to hear. *He's a sweetie?* Jake had Molly totally brainwashed.

"Too bad I lost interest. I mean, he was great, but I needed to be with someone who wasn't so passive and everything."

Oh, for the love of all that's good and holy.

"Shit!" Molly shouted again. "Jessica and I were supposed to met Jim on the tennis court twenty minutes ago. Talk later, bye!"

Cordelia hung up her phone and banged her head against her desk until she got her frustration out, which amounted to one minute, twenty-nine seconds (she timed it on her Swatch). All the reservations were made. Everything was set in place. But Cordelia couldn't help but feel like she had just signed a contract with the spawn of Satan. She was going to drive to Eureka with Jake Stein and when she finally got there, she'd be spending two months with Molly, who was apparently ten times flightier.

She missed Paul now more than ever before, so she grabbed her Treo and sent him a text message.

COUNTING DOWN THE DAYS. XOXO

Chapter Three

Cordelia was fuming. For the zillionth time that Tuesday, she looked at her Swatch. It was almost four o'clock. Four o'clock! She'd been waiting for Jacob Stein since ten that morning, the mutually agreed-upon time of departure.

Not that this was surprising. Jake's irresponsible streak had reared its nasty head about a month into his and Molly's relationship. One night, Jake and Molly had had plans to go to a house party, and Cordelia had asked if they could drop her at Alexis Dunbar's place. She'd wanted to get there by eight to watch a *Practice* marathon, and Jake had known that. But once it was time to go, he'd kept dillydallying. He'd chatted with her father about blues guitarists and had gone into the kitchen every five minutes for a cup of her mom's fresh-brewed Arabica coffee. When they had finally gotten in the car at nine thirty P.M., Jake had had to run back into the house to use the bathroom.

That kind of thing was typical with Jake, and Cordelia growled at the thought of it. Especially because it was happening once again.

At eleven this morning, Jake had called to tell her he was having a little car trouble—nothing major, but he had to take it to the garage and would be by to pick her up within the hour. When he didn't show up at noon, she'd called his cell phone, and Jake had said that he had to go home because he forgot to pack his drum-sticks. At one, she'd called again, and his exact words were: "Stop stalking me." Then he hung up. When she called at three, three fifteen, and three thirty, he didn't even answer.

Suddenly, she felt the pulsating buzz of her Treo. Cordelia could barely contain her irritation when she saw Jake's name appear.

"Do you have *any* concept of time?" she said through clenched teeth.

He didn't sound the least bit distraught. "About as much as Sir Sandford Fleming did."

Cordelia was confused. "What are you talking about?"

"Sir Sandford Fleming. Head of the International

Prime Meridian Conference of 1884. C'mon, Cordelia, an egghead like you should know simple facts like that."

Before she could come back with a witty response, he spoke again.

"Turning onto your street. You ready?"

"I've been ready for six hours," she replied, and hung up. If she had talked any longer, she might have said something really insulting, and Cordelia had vowed around two o'clock that she was going to take the moral high road. She was not—repeat, *was not*—going to stoop to Jacob Stein's level. Nothing he could say or do would get her to lose her cool. Cordelia Packer was going to be unflappable on this trip. Or else she might end up doing something that could get her shipped off to Alcatraz.

Cordelia went to the living room window to watch for Jake's arrival. Her parents had waited around for a couple of hours in the morning, but then her father had to get to a can't-miss meeting at his ad agency. Her mom had an obligation too—she was prepping for this big Red Cross fund-raiser—so she'd told Cordelia to give Jake a hug hello for them. Cordelia had to fight the urge to gag.

That urge returned the moment a beat-up-looking car with a bumper sticker that read, GIVE ME AMBIGUITY OR GIVE ME SOMETHING ELSE, pulled into the driveway. She shook her head in disbelief. Jake had driven an SUV when he was dating Molly, but apparently he had traded it in for a crappy tin can that desperately needed a house call from the *Pimp My Ride* crew. Cordelia pushed her face up against the glass and tried to get a better look. Was that duct tape on the passenger seat? And were all the tires spares? Not only was this trip going to be unbearable emotionally, but it also looked like it was going to be uncomfortable physically. Greyhound never sounded so good.

Cordelia was startled when a loud, drawn-out horn sounded from outside. It shook the entire house almost as much as the 3.1-sized earthquake that hit last year.

There is no way I'm moving, she thought as she looked over to her pile of bags. She knew she had to set some standards right at the beginning and Jake had to know immediately that she did not respond to car horns or whistles or whatever. She experienced a quick moment of satisfaction as he finally got out of the car. Then something else struck her—hard.

Jacob Stein had miraculously transformed into a drool-inducing, yummy piece of eye candy. As he closed in on the house, Cordelia concentrated on every new, smoldering feature of Jake's. He'd cut his long hair so that it was shorter and layered in a way that framed his face, which was looking pretty damn fine. Jake's skin had this healthy glow that radiated like no guy's skin had a right to. Cordelia could see his blue eyes shimmering through the afternoon haze. Jake must have had a growth spurt, too, because now he stood tall and lean like Paul did.

Talk about pimp my ride! she thought. *He's like a totally different person.*

Then as soon as Cordelia opened the door, Jake opened his mouth and ruined everything.

"Didn't you hear me honking?" he barked.

"Yes, I heard you," she replied coolly. "In fact, all of San Diego heard you. Even the dead people."

Jake crossed his arms. "Well, then, why are you just standing here?"

Cordelia was distracted by his biceps for a second and then snapped to attention. "I was waiting for you to come and help me with my bags."

Jake did a double take when he looked at her luggage. "You're taking all *that*? I don't know if there's enough space in my trunk."

"I'm staying in Eureka all summer," she reminded him. "Besides, I thought you had an SUV."

"That was my father's," he replied. He gestured grandly toward the heap of metal parked in the driveway. "*This* is all mine. An '82 Dodge Charger. Just got it last month."

"Congratulations," she said snidely. "It's very…you."

Jake still beamed with pride. "I know, it's great."

Cordelia rolled her eyes. Apparently Jake and Molly were both delusional.

Despite what he'd said, Jake helped Cordelia with her stuff, and they managed to squeeze everything into the trunk.

Cordelia opened the passenger door and looked inside. The entire contents of a garbage can appeared to be stuck to the bottom of the car floor. She sighed at the sight of it, but then she glanced at her watch and began to feel a sensation of panic rising inside her chest. This happened every time things weren't going according to plan. In addition to the nervous stomach symptoms, Cordelia often experienced shortness of breath. She knew she had to calm down, but that was so hard to do when Jake Stein was within one hundred yards of her. She figured that when they got on the road, she'd be less stressed, so she decided to give Jake another nudge.

"We're getting a very late start and I want to be in San Luis Obispo by at least eight, so we should probably hurry up and head out now." She had made an appointment for an evening massage at the hotel spa and didn't want to miss it.

He took out a rag from his back pocket and wiped the crushed bugs off the front windshield. "San Luis Obispo? Are you nuts?"

"Didn't you look at the itinerary I sent you?"

"Yeah, sure, but San Luis Obispo, that's like five hours from here." He threw the rag in the backseat. Cordelia winced when it landed on her makeup bag.

"This baby's running okay now, but I'm not pushing her past fifty."

"You've got to be kidding."

Jake got into the car and patted the dashboard. "It'll be fine. Trust me."

She realized just how hard trusting Jake was going to be the second he tried to start the car. It took Jake three attempts before the engine finally made a sputtering noise. Just when she thought that Jake should put a Do Not Resuscitate order on his car, she heard an ominous thump.

Cordelia shuddered. "What was *that*?"

"Probably the muffler falling out."

She shot him a glare.

He grinned. "Just kidding."

That so-called sense of humor of his is so not *funny*, she thought as she sank back in her seat, trying to ignore whatever was poking her from beneath the ripped upholstery. (She really didn't want to know.)

As Jake began to make his way through town, Cordelia pulled out her Treo and brought up the itinerary. Studying it, she wondered if they could make up the lost time, or if she should add another day to the trip.

"Where can we get to in a couple of hours?" Jake asked. "LA? Santa Barbara? I'm really beat from all those errands today."

Cordelia huffed. "Errands? You call going home for

your drumsticks 'errands'?"

"They're just as important as that little gadget of yours," Jake said as he looked over her shoulder. "God, Cordy, did you really have to make lists of all the rest stops with handicap accessible bathrooms?"

Cordelia pulled the Treo to her chest. "Keep your eyes on the road!"

Jake let out a booming laugh, one that she found surprisingly infectious. She couldn't help but smile.

"I like the roomier stalls, okay?" she explained.

"I'm sure you do," he said.

Then Jake suddenly made a sharp right hand turn, practically throwing Cordelia against the door.

"This seat belt's loose!" she yelled.

He shrugged. "Nobody's perfect."

The car screeched to a halt in front of a 7-Eleven.

Cordelia tried to catch her breath. "Why are we stopping already?"

"I need to get gas. And I'm hungry. Want anything?"

She thought about her pledge to Paul that she would eat more vegetables. *Would Lay's potato chips and veggie dip qualify?*

Other thoughts of Paul began to drift into her mind. His bright smile, his perpetual good mood, his gentle nature…

Suddenly, Jake snapped his fingers in front of her face.

Cordelia couldn't believe how rude he was being.

"Don't snap at me, okay?"

"Then tell me what you want."

"Um, a bag of Veggie Booty," she said. "And a Snapple Diet Peach Iced Tea."

"That's it?" he asked.

And a jumbo-size bottle of Excedrin.

"Yep, that's it."

He shrugged and got out of the car.

Cordelia wrung her hands and bounced her left leg up and down for the next twenty minutes. She couldn't believe Jake was taking so long. What could he possibly be doing? The only thing she could think of was armed robbery, but even if that were true, he was definitely the slowest criminal in the history of convenience store knock-overs.

After ten more minutes of being MIA, Jake appeared with a huge container of cheese puffs under one arm and a gallon of caffeine-free Dr Pepper under the other. Jake threw the items in the backseat and hopped in the car. "Sorry, they didn't have the stuff you wanted. Hope that's close enough."

Cordelia felt her face get hot. "It took you a half hour to buy *two* things?"

He tried to start the car, but the engine just coughed. "Your fixation on time is really unhealthy, you know that?"

"What took you so long?" she asked.

"The craziest thing happened," Jake replied as he jiggled the key in the ignition. "The cashier dude and I were in first grade together. Haven't seen him since he transferred to this private school. Man, did he bulk up. He was this skinny beanpole a long time ago. I'm surprised I recognized him."

The car began to rattle once it started.

"That's incredible, Jake. I'll alert the media," Cordelia said wryly.

"Are you going to be in a bad mood for the entire trip?" he asked. "Oh, I forgot. This is your *regular* mood."

Cordelia leaned back in her seat and gazed out the window sullenly. Paul would never have said something that mean. "Whatever. Just drive, okay?" The tiny wheels of the Charger spun around, and Jake peeled out into the street.

Her heart started to thump as she peeked at the gas gauge, which was practically on empty. "Hey, I thought you needed to get gas."

Jake rolled up the window a bit and then it jammed. He didn't try to force it any farther. "Did you see those prices? Over two bucks a gallon. Do me a favor and keep an eye out for places that sell unleaded fuel for under two."

Cordelia was twitching now. Jake wasn't thinking this strategy through very well and it was making her anxious. "But what if we run out before then? That red needle is on the E."

He patted the dashboard. "She'll hang in there. Don't worry."

"And what if she doesn't? What's your Plan B?" she asked nervously.

"Plan B is whatever the hell we come up with later," he replied nonchalantly.

This kind of logic *really* blew Cordelia's mind, mostly because it wasn't logic at all. It was completely nonsensical.

Cordelia tried to close her eyes and think happy thoughts of Paul. If she ever needed to figure out how to meditate, now was the time. What were his instructions again? *Find my center and then visualize something tranquil. But was that before or after I began the rhythmic breathing?* She wanted to follow these steps to inner peace precisely, but the collective sound of multiple cars honking made her snap out of her attempt at meditation.

Cordelia glanced over at Jake, who was staring straight ahead and frowning. "Rush hour," he announced.

They were bumper-to-bumper in a line of cars that looked like it stretched on forever. It was five o'clock, and they weren't even out of San Diego. Consider the massage out of the question. In fact, the whole itinerary might be affected because of this snafu.

"If we'd left when we were supposed to, we'd be in

San Luis Obispo right now," she stated.

Jake did that "who cares" shoulder-shrug thing again. "Well, we didn't, so we're not."

He then proceeded to get out of his seat, lean over toward the back, and stick his butt (which just happened to be incredibly toned) in her face before plopping back down in front of the steering wheel. He put the cheese puffs container in between his legs and began to devour them.

Cordelia couldn't believe that she'd only been with Jake for a little less than an hour and she was already bargaining with God for some sort of transporter-beam miracle.

Jake poked Cordelia in the shoulder and held out a handful of cheese puffs. "Want some?"

She could see that some of the orange stuff was embedded beneath his fingernails and immediately lost her appetite. "I had a big lunch, so I'm fine."

With this shrug, his shoulders practically met his earlobes. "More for me."

Cordelia tried to hide the fact that her hands were trembling as she pulled her iPod out from her bag. Just as she was about to put her headphones on and tune everything out, Jake poked her again.

"Could you stop with the poking, please?"

"I poke because I care," Jake retorted.

He is so *annoying!*

"Did you want something?" she asked.

Jake grimaced. "Yeah, I got one of those adapters for my iPod. It runs through the tape deck. Want to plug yours in?"

All right, this is borderline thoughtful of him, Cordelia thought. *He's trying to do something to make me comfortable, so I better take him up on it. It could be the last nice thing he does.*

"Yeah, that would be great. Thanks."

She hooked up the adapter to her iPod and turned it on. The volume was very loud, which was a relief. It would drown out the rush-hour noise and prevent them from having any more hostile conversations. Cordelia began to sway to the music and smile a little bit. Then she turned to look at Jake, who had gone completely pale.

"IS THAT THE BACKSTREET BOYS?" he screamed.

Cordelia pretended not to hear him. "HEY, YOU! NO BACKSTREET BOYS!" he shouted again.

She sighed and turned it off. 'Incomplete' happens to be a hit song, Jake. If that bothers you, take it up with Ryan Seacrest or something."

He groaned. "It's a whole lotta commercial crap, that's what it is."

"Just because it's popular doesn't make it bad," she declared.

"Sure it does."

Cordelia knew that she should pull out her headphones again and be the bigger person here. But she couldn't let Jake get away with acting like he knew what quality music was while insinuating that the rest of the country were a bunch of idiots. "Then put on something *you* like. I can't wait to hear what you consider music."

Jake reached over Cordelia, opened up the glove compartment, and pulled out his MP3 player. She shied away to give him some room, but his right elbow and upper arm brushed against her left breast a little. A millisecond later, her stomach fluttered and her skin was covered in goose bumps.

Holy shit, what was that?

She didn't have time to analyze this strange reaction at all because a melancholy, almost whiny tune that she'd never heard before filled the car. It was one of those alt-rock songs that examines the shape of a poppy seed and then uses that as a metaphor for how people should look at life. Jake slapped his hand against his thigh (also well-toned) in time to the music, just as if he were playing drums in the band.

"It's Pedro the Lion. They're from Seattle. I'm going to check them out there, maybe write an article and try to sell it to *Rolling Stone*."

She nodded politely. She had challenged him to this music duel so that she could shut him down, but now she was reconsidering it. Her body was doing some strange stuff and she didn't want to make it worse.

"What do you think of them?" he asked.

She simply shrugged.

Jake seemed to be determined to get some kind of response out of her. "You don't like that kind of music, huh?"

"It's...listenable," she replied. "The melody is nice."

He made a snorting sound. "These guys are geniuses. I bet if you just...unwound yourself a little, you'd be able to appreciate them like I do."

Cordelia burst out laughing. "Gimme a break. I can unwind just fine to Nick Carter, thank you very much."

"Right, well, you'll do whatever is safe, Cordy," Jake said pompously.

Cordelia was stunned. The nerve of this guy! He barely even knew her and here he was making comments about her music choices as if they represented who she was.

"So you like Pedro the Lion and that means you're laid-back and enlightened," she retorted. "But because I like the Backstreet Boys, I'm an uptight pansy?"

As soon as she said that, she heard another tune, a recognizable one this time. It turned out to be the ring tone of Jake's cell.

The conversation he had with whoever was on the other end wasn't interesting—it was all "yeah," "no," "okay"—but she was intrigued by something else.

"Your ring tone," she said after he hung up. "That

was OutKast, right? 'Jazzy Belle'?"

"Yeah."

She smiled. "That's *commercial crap*, if you ask me."

Jake didn't respond. He just shut off the music and stared ahead at the traffic, which was barely inching along. Cordelia then noticed something very unusual. She was really, *really* relaxed, almost peaceful even. Car horns were still blaring all around her, yet she had managed to find her center, like Paul had always said she would.

She just thought it was rather odd that the only reason she'd stumbled upon it was because she'd shut Jacob Stein up.

Chapter Four

Cordelia and Jake managed to get out of the traffic jam in about two hours without beating each other into a bloody pulp. In fact, Cordelia had been so chill the entire time, it seemed to be making Jake nervous. He kept moaning whenever they passed a speed limit sign and he realized that the Charger wasn't traveling above thirty miles per hour. She couldn't help but giggle a little. It was rather enjoyable to see Jake sweating the small stuff, considering how "wound-up" he thought she was and how "loose" he claimed to be.

But once they started whizzing past other cars, Cordelia's nerves began to resurface. "Hey, I thought you weren't going to push this thing past fifty?"

Jake smirked as he accelerated even further. "Well, I

don't want to ruin that precious schedule of yours. The whole world might come to an end."

Cordelia looked at her Swatch. "It's only seven thirty," she said. "We can make it to Santa Barbara tonight. There's no need to rush."

Just then the car started shaking violently. She swore the Charger was having some sort of Jake-induced seizure, much like she would if this heap of metal died on the side of the road.

"Now what?" she asked.

Steam wafted up from underneath the hood.

Jake scratched his head. "Uh, looks like it's overheating."

He hit the turn signal and got into the right lane, then pulled off at an exit that was taking them right into a not-so-great section of Los Angeles.

Cordelia had never felt so helpless in her life. This situation was getting out of control. What made things worse was that Jake didn't appear to be the least bit bothered by it. He was acting as if this was just a normal day for him. Cordelia couldn't be more put off by his "whatev" attitude. It was exasperating.

"All we need to do is let her rest overnight and we'll be fine," Jake explained. "That traffic really did a number on her."

Cordelia rolled her eyes. "I'm sure she's exhausted."

"Why do you have to be like that?" Jake snapped.

"Why do you have to talk about your car like it's a *person*?"

"Forget it," he said with a huff.

"I don't understand why we just don't have a mechanic look at it," she prodded. "That makes the most sense."

"Well, I don't trust mechanics. They always rip you off," he replied. "I've done this before, okay? Tomorrow morning she'll be good as new."

Cordelia crossed her arms in front of her chest and set her eyes on the graffiti-covered storefronts that were passing by her window. Then she felt a firm nudge to her ribs.

ARGH!!!

Cordelia spun around and nudged Jake back. "Quit it!" she shrieked.

He reacted by pointing to a neon sign declaring VA AN IES and a shabby motel, ironically dubbed the Renaissance. "We can stay there," he announced.

As soon as she noticed that the motel was located in between an adult video store and a seedy pool hall, Cordelia's heart jumped into her throat. "No, we can't."

"Why not?"

"It doesn't look…safe."

"Right, you and your safety issues," Jake growled as he pulled into the parking lot. "C'mon, Cordy. It says on the sign that it's AAA recommended. Would AAA steer us wrong?"

Cordelia shook her head. "Sorry, I'm not staying there."

Jake muttered something under his breath and began driving around. "What about this one?"

Cordelia winced. "You see those ladies standing on the corner? This motel rents *by the hour*."

Jake furrowed his brow in frustration. Cordelia tried to prevent herself from laughing. It was a rare thing to see Jake so tense and agitated. Actually, it kind of made him a little bit...cute.

Suddenly the smoking car screeched to a halt in front of a Holiday Inn Express. The "Service Engine Soon" light was flickering like a firefly.

"We're staying here and that's that," Jake said as he turned the Charger off.

"I don't see any vacancy sign," Cordelia said.

He gave her a hard stare. "Is this the face of someone who cares?"

"I'll see if there are any rooms available," Cordelia said, and jumped out. Inside the registration office, she noted with approval the tidy reception area with its modern, tasteful furniture and the business-suit-clad man behind the desk. This was definitely a million times better than the Renaissance. She could finally rest easy.

"May I help you?" he asked.

"Do you have two rooms for tonight?"

"There are a lot of people here for a wedding, so we only have one room left. It has a queen-size bed. Will that do?"

So much for resting easy. Cordelia's palms began to sweat the moment the man said "one room left," and now that he had said "queen-size bed," her legs had turned into pudding.

"I'll be right back," she told him.

On the walk back to Jake's car, she carefully played the situation out in her mind. She and Jake could share the room and sleep in the same bed—it could all be very innocent. He'd have his half of the mattress; she'd stay on hers. Nothing would happen and her virginity would stay intact for Paul (whom she had to call the second she had a moment to herself). But knowing Jake—and Cordelia felt like she knew him better than anyone—he probably snored like a Saint Bernard and hogged the covers and did other insanely annoying things that would keep her awake all night long and make her miserable.

When Cordelia approached the driver's-side window, she swallowed hard. Jake had managed to roll the window up while she was gone, but now he couldn't get it to go down again, so he just opened the door. She was taken aback when their eyes met. He seemed so harmless as he sat there, drumsticks in his hands, hair messed up from the slight breeze that was in the air (or was that smog?). There was even a hint of kindness in his crooked smile. What on earth was going through that mind of his? She wasn't sure she wanted to know. But then again, there was something inside of her that was very, very curious.

"So here's the deal," she said firmly. "There's one room with one bed."

Jake snickered and beat on the door with his sticks. "That's what they all say."

Cordelia sneered at him. She wanted to shove that fleeting curiosity of hers right up his ass. "Dream on, Jake."

"I'm kidding, Cordy. Lighten up."

She hated it when he made comments like that. She *wasn't* uptight. *He* was the one with the problem. *He* was the one who was just about as aggravating as a hemorrhoid.

"So do you want to share it with me or not?" she asked.

He got out of the car and stretched. His T-shirt pulled up so that Cordelia could see his abs. They were really flat—not six-pack status, but definitely rock hard. There was even this small patch of hair that went from his belly button down to the waistline of his low-slung black jeans.

"Nah, that's okay, you can take the room," he said with a yawn. "I snore really loud and all that shit, so I'll sleep in the car."

Cordelia smiled. She'd been right about Jake more than once today. But she didn't expect him to be so generous and give up a room in a hotel, especially after sitting in a car for a few hours.

"Maybe we should try another hotel."

"That's okay. I'd rather yield to the needs of the Charger."

She stood there uncertainly. "You're sure?"

"Yeah, I've done it before. It's not a problem."

She glanced at the backseat. It was pretty wide, but he wouldn't be able to stretch out. Then she remembered the odd neighborhood they were in. Would he even be safe in the Charger all by himself?

"Are you going to be okay in there, though? What if somebody bothers you?"

Jake put his drumsticks into his back pocket, then suddenly grabbed both her arms and yanked her quickly so that she was pressed up against his torso. Cordelia yelped as he squeezed her tightly, and her heart was pounding as if she'd just run with the bulls in Pamplona, Spain.

"I can take care of myself," he said, his mouth dangerously close to her right ear. "And whoever else is looking for trouble."

Cordelia laughed nervously. "All right, Jake. Ease up on the judo, okay?"

He grimaced. "Surprised you, didn't I?"

She grinned right back at him. "I guess."

"What if I helped you with your bags? Would that totally floor you?"

"Let's find out," Cordelia said mischievously.

They walked around to the back of the car and Jake popped the trunk. She went for a heavy bag, but he tapped her on the shoulder and shook his head before lugging it down to the reservation office himself. This time, she didn't feel annoyed by his touch. Maybe it was because he was being nice. Maybe it was because they were tired. Maybe it was how the warm California sun was lighting up the clear indigo sky.

Whatever the reason, it seemed as if Jake might be letting his guard down for a change. And if that were the case, maybe they'd actually be able to get along for the next few days. Then a strange thought entered Cordelia's mind.

Maybe we'll even turn out to be friends.

*   *   *

A few minutes later, a nice motel worker showed Cordelia how to adjust the temperature and shut the blinds in her room. She tipped him two dollars and closed the door behind him.

The place wasn't bad at all. It was spotlessly clean. There was a small TV that had HBO (since *The Practice* had been canceled, Cordelia's favorite show was *Rome*) and a mini-refrigerator that had a few complimentary sodas in it. And one gigantic bed with a mountain of fluffy pillows.

She contemplated the bed and bit her lower lip. Then she went to the window, lifted a slat of the blind, and peered out. Jake was parked out in front of her room. It was too dark to see inside the car, but she assumed he'd already settled down in the backseat. She could picture him, curled up in the fetal position on the ripped upholstery, among the black plastic trash bags that he had referred to as "my matching luggage set." While she had this enormous bed that could fit the two of them and the rest of LA.

Cordelia dropped the blind once she heard her Treo chirping. She dashed across the room and fetched it off the coffee table. The caller ID read: *BBE* (Best Boyfriend Ever).

"I am *so* happy that you called," she said as soon as she picked up.

"Really?"

Cordelia practically melted at the sound of his voice. "You have no idea."

Paul chuckled. "That bad, huh?"

"Well, because Jake was late picking me up today, I had to chuck my itinerary out the window. I had to cancel my hotel reservations, so now there's not even a basic plan in place." She sighed.

"Wow, that's unprecedented," he replied.

"And that car of his. It should be condemned! We're at this Holiday Inn Express in Los Angeles so that it can cool off or something."

"Are you guys sharing a room?" Paul sounded concerned, which Cordelia thought was so sweet.

"No, there was only one room and I got it. Jake is staying in his car," she assured him.

"Well, that's very gentlemanly. He can't be all that bad," he said.

Cordelia knew that Paul was absolutely right. Jake *wasn't* all bad. Perhaps he was even somewhat okay, once you got past his many, *many* irritating qualities.

"He's just...a handful, that's all."

Paul laughed heartily. "So are you, Cordy."

Hold on. What? She took a little offense to this. Sure, she had her quirks, but she wasn't anything remotely close to Jake. "Uh, I'm just organized and structured. There's nothing wrong with that."

"Of course there isn't. It's just that, you know, you're kind of...how shall I put this?" There was a long, awkward pause as Paul searched for the right phrase. "I got it. High maintenance."

Cordelia felt like she had just been hit in the teeth with a sledgehammer. She wasn't used to Paul flinging labels around like that. He hadn't called her a slut or a retard or anything, but whatever. For some reason, what he'd said seemed just as bad. "High maintenance? *High maintenance?*"

"What'd I say?" Paul said uneasily.

The quiver in his voice made Cordelia worry that she was overreacting, and who was she kidding? She probably was. She tried to do that breathing thing again and regain her composure.

"Well, nothing, it's just that I thought you liked how I...stuck to my principles," she said calmly.

"I do, Cordy. I didn't mean to...wait, hold on a sec?"

"Yeah, okay."

Cordelia sulked as she waited for Paul to come back. High maintenance. That had a negative connotation, right? It meant rigid and strict and uptight. It's how Jake would describe her. And maybe even Molly would too. Paul was supposed to think she was some charming eccentric, and that she was brilliant like that guy in *A Beautiful Mind*, only not schizophrenic.

"I'm back."

"Hi," she whimpered.

"Listen, forget about what I said. I think you're wonderful," he said softly.

This perked her up a little bit. "Go on."

She could feel Paul smiling on the other end. "And incredibly gorgeous," he added.

"Anything else?"

"Um...yeah. I really wish you were here. Yosemite is

so invigorating. There's all this wildlife and these enormous trees." Then suddenly his voice got low and raspy. "God, I wish I was kissing you right now."

Oh, I like where this is going, she said to herself.

RING! RING! RING!

The telephone in the room completely startled her.

"Hold that thought," she told Paul. Then she leaped over to the phone and picked it up. "Hello?"

"Do you have any Listerine in there? My breath is rank."

F'ing Jake.

"Your breath is fine," Cordelia snapped.

"There's a nasty taste in my mouth. I just need to rinse it out."

"I'm busy right now. Can't this wait?"

"It'll only take a second," he said.

"Just call back in a few minutes."

"What are you doing in there?"

Cordelia kept looking at her Treo. She wanted to kill Jake for interrupting what would have been her first sexy phone call with her amazing, minty-fresh-breathed boyfriend. "I'm talking with Paul."

Suddenly Jake burst into a fit of laughter.

"What's so funny?" she asked angrily.

"Nothing," he said. "Catch you later." Now the only thing Cordelia was in the mood to do was bash skulls.

She picked up her Treo and tried to calm down. "Hey, I'm back."

"Sorry, Cordy, I've got to go. Stewart and I are going to go to an Eco Warrior info meeting."

Cordelia practically crushed the Treo in her hand in disappointment. "Oh, okay. Have a good time."

"Thanks, we'll talk tomorrow," Paul said. "Miss you."

"Miss you too," she replied. "Bye."

The next thing Cordelia did was lock herself in the bathroom with all of her favorite products and soak her bitterness away in the tub. When the water began to cool and her skin began to prune, she got out. Feeling light and delicate, she patted herself dry and smoothed on some Elizabeth Arden Green Tea body lotion. She was pretty much back to normal.

Cordelia slipped into her pink satin cami and boxers from Victoria's Secret and decided to settle down with a good book—she'd bought *Peaches*, a novel about three girls who become friends while spending a summer at a Georgia peach orchard. She was really excited to dive into it.

After an hour of reading, her eyes began to feel heavy, so she put the book aside, turned off the light, and closed her eyes.

But moments later, they sprang open. Cordelia rolled over onto her stomach and closed her eyes again. After forty-five minutes, she hadn't fallen asleep. She tried lying on her side—it didn't work. Then she sat up and turned the light back on.

Okay, what is this all about? Cordelia thought. She had expected sleep to wash over her immediately, but it hadn't happened. Was she still too wound up over her conversation with Paul? Was she expecting Jake to bother her about Q-tips any second? No, it was something else that kept her from sleeping. And Cordelia couldn't bear to admit it, but it was true. She was feeling a little bit...guilty.

She was lying there in a comfortable room and Jake was scrunched up in the backseat of a car because he didn't want to put her out. Yes, he was extremely annoying to be around and he drove her nuts, but she knew the temperature dropped at night and he didn't even have a blanket out there with him. It just wasn't right.

She thought about what Paul had said earlier. Maybe it was possible that she was also a bit...*much* at times. Was that any reason to subject Jake to the elements? And she was still worried that someone would try to mess with him. He was a young guy alone in his car and he was vulnerable. Cordelia couldn't believe this. She was actually feeling protective of him.

She got out of bed, went to the window, and peeked through the blinds again. She couldn't see anything. He could already be dead in that car.

And it would be your fault for letting him sleep out there, she told herself.

Cordelia went to the motel room door and opened

it. It was cool out, but it would only take a second for her to dash over to the car window and peek in, just to make sure he was okay. Hell, she might even ask him to come inside and crash on the floor.

She glanced around and made sure there was no one outside to see her. Then she slipped out and hurried over to the Charger. Pressing her face against the back window, she could see Jake clearly. He was sound asleep, and as she watched, she could see his chest rising and falling. He was absolutely fine. In fact, he looked rather timid lying there. There was this small smirk on his face, too. Not the usual obnoxious kind, but a happy one, like he was dreaming of something really pleasant. And then she noticed something else. He wasn't snoring at all. He wasn't even a heavy breather. Jake had obviously made it all up so she could have the room to herself.

Why would he do that?

All of a sudden, there was a clattering noise that came from behind Cordelia and spooked her. She scampered back to her room, put her hand on the doorknob, and turned it. That is, *tried* to turn it. The handle didn't budge. A very familiar sick feeling rose up inside her. She had done something completely stupid. She'd locked herself out.

Holy shit!

She went to the window, but there was no way to open it. Then she tried the handle again.

Looking down toward the registration office, Cordelia willed the person inside to come out and help her. Of course, nothing happened. She was going to have to walk over there. In her pink satin Victoria's Secret cami and boxers. Which were practically transparent.

And as her luck would have it, the manager wasn't alone in the office. Three men were in the process of checking in. Once they got a good look at her, they probably thought she came with one of the pricier rooms.

Cordelia folded her arms across her chest and tried to speak with dignity, but it was hopeless. She was utterly humiliated. She couldn't help but think that Molly would have never let herself get into this situation. And even if she had, she would have been unshaken by it. That's the kind of confidence her sister had possessed since she was a toddler. That's the reason boys like Jake—hell, *all* boys—were really drawn to Molly. Well, that and her perky, grapefruit-sized breasts.

Cordelia swallowed hard before speaking and looked down at her feet. "Uh, sir? I locked myself out of my room. Can I have another key?"

"Just a moment," the manager said. "Mary? Would you help this guest?"

Mary turned out to be a middle-aged, gray-haired lady who was sporting a huge pair of knockoff Gucci sunglasses. She thought that was rather weird considering the sun had gone down hours ago, and the woman was working at a Holiday Inn Express, not a fashion show runway. Mary came out from some inner office, took one look at Cordelia, pursed her lips, and raised her eyebrows.

"I locked myself out of my room," Cordelia repeated shyly.

One of the men snickered. Then the registration office door opened. A tired-looking man and woman came in with suitcases and a small child.

"Look, Mommy! That girl is in her undies!" the kid piped up.

At least *that* comment got Mary moving. She snatched up a key. "Come along," she barked at Cordelia.

With her arms still folded across her chest, Cordelia ducked her head down and followed her outside. They had almost reached the room without further incident when she heard a faint but familiar sound.

She looked up and saw Jake doubled over in laughter so hard that the Charger was rocking back and forth. He tried to roll the window down again, probably in the hopes of shouting out some snide remark that would make her feel far worse than she already did.

Forget about being friends! This guy will never be anything but a gigantic pain in my ass.

Fortunately, Mary opened the door just as Jake's window came down. Cordelia thanked her quickly, then ducked inside the room and closed the door. She dashed across the room and dove back into bed. Burying her face in the pillow, she pulled the sheets and blanket over her head.

But even like that, Cordelia swore she could still hear Jake laughing.

Chapter Five

Cordelia didn't get a wink of sleep that night. She tossed and turned until the sun came up, which was the most awful feeling in the world. When she went to the bathroom and looked in the mirror, she could barely recognize the gnarly creature staring back at her. The whites of her eyes were now a gross pink color. Her skin was peeling and she hadn't even spent one glorious day on the beach in a week. Her hair seemed stringy and frayed at the ends, but she'd just gotten a hot oil treatment and a trim a few days ago. Her haggard appearance could only be attributed to one thing and one thing only: She was having a nervous breakdown brought on by too much Jacob Stein exposure.

She had considered calling her parents and asking

them to rescue her, but that would only create a big stir and then Molly might get upset at her. She would just have to bite the bullet, so to speak, and pray that she would make it to Eureka before she really cracked.

Cordelia got into Jake's car without saying a word. Apparently he was right about the Charger. Once he started her up, she purred like she had just gotten back from vacation. A few minutes later, Cordelia could feel Jake's eyes on her as the car sputtered along the highway, but she refused to look at him. She had a feeling that the moment she did, he'd break into another laughing fit and then she'd be forced to throw him from the moving vehicle.

"Jazzy Belle" rang out and Jake picked up his phone. "Yeah?"

Cordelia was about to mention to Jake that it was illegal and dangerous to talk on a cell phone while driving, but that would mean speaking to him. At this point in time, she'd rather risk a grisly accident. Maybe that would put her out of her misery.

"Okay, yeah, right. Bye."

He tossed it back on the seat, but within seconds OutKast was playing once again. Cordelia couldn't believe that even Jake's cell phone had the ability to get on her nerves. She was certain that she was losing it. She needed to find that center of hers and quick.

"Yeah. Nah, later. Huh? Okay," he said in monotone.

She kept her eyes focused straight ahead and prepared to grab the wheel from his hands if he swerved while talking. Jake didn't strike her as the kind of person who could multitask well. There were countless pieces of evidence, like the time he had tried to drink a can of soda while showing Molly how to slam dance and proceeded to spill the entire contents onto her mother's precious white living room carpet. Or the time when he had dinged her father's BMW convertible because he was reading *Mad* magazine as he drove into the driveway. The funny thing was, the only person who ever got upset about these incidents was Cordelia.

Oh my God, she thought. *I am the poster child for the High Maintenance Federation.*

But did that make Jake any less infuriating?

Cordelia went against her better judgment and turned to look at him.

"Didn't sleep too well, huh?" he asked with a wicked grin.

The answer to the previous question was a resounding N-O.

Lack of sleep, Jake's wisecrack, and yet another ring of his cell phone had resulted in a nasty headache that Cordelia couldn't shake. She leaned back, closed her eyes, and tried to focus her mind on the positive, which of course meant thinking about Paul. They had talked again that morning and made plans to meet up later in the afternoon. Cordelia hadn't reminded Jake about it just yet, because he'd most likely give her attitude and she didn't want to deal with that right now. So she decided that once he stopped to fuel up, she'd try and charm him over. Hey, she was sisters with *the* Molly Packer. Some of that magical charisma had to be hiding in Cordelia's genetic makeup. Paul had fallen for the littlest Packer, after all.

Cordelia wrapped her arms around her stomach, which was churning as much as her head was pounding. She missed Paul even more than she thought she would. Maybe this was because she'd been stuck here with Jake the Human Ass-Bite, so Paul seemed that much more incredible. Nah. Paul was amazing in his own right. Even though he'd thrown her a bit in their chat last evening, he was usually so sweet and grounded and…normal.

Eventually, the rhythmic sound of the Charger driving over the seams in the highway helped Cordelia to nod off to sleep. She even dreamed that she was at Yosemite and Paul was at the top of a giant sequoia. He kept asking her to join him up there so they could drink mango juice and talk to a monkey named Earl. Cordelia grabbed a branch and tried to hoist herself up, but her legs were so heavy, she could barely raise them. When she looked down, she noticed that she was submerged in a quicksand made of cheese puffs and she was sinking. Then she glanced up and Jake was standing on the branch she was holding. He kept jumping on it and suddenly it catapulted her up into the part of the tree where Paul was talking with Earl the monkey. Earl, who spoke with a British accent, insisted she board a plane that was made out of coconuts. Once she was seated and it took off, she noticed how high up she was and that there was no pilot. Then she began to scream.

In fact, Cordelia screamed herself wide awake, much to Jake's horror.

"Jesus Christ!" he shouted.

She was panting heavily and sweating like the time when Molly had forgotten that Cordelia was using the sauna and locked her in there for twenty minutes.

"God, Cordy. Are you okay?" Jake asked in concern.

"Yeah, I just had a nightmare."

Cordelia checked her Swatch and saw that she'd slept for two hours. They ought to be right around Bakersfield by now, but then again, she had fallen asleep before reminding Jake that they were supposed to stop in Yosemite this afternoon, so who knows where he had taken them.

"Where are we?" she asked.

"We're on I-15," he replied.

Cordelia scrambled for her bag, reached in, and found her Treo. She pulled up her map on the screen and studied it furiously.

"Wait, Jake, we're supposed to be on I-5."

She had a bad feeling about this.

"Well I-5 isn't going to get us to Las Vegas."

Cordelia felt another nuclear explosion-like scream building within her. "I'm sorry. I must still be asleep and having that nightmare. I thought you said we were going to Las Vegas."

"Yeah, I forgot to tell you. I need to stop there because I left some important stuff at my ex-roommate's place and I gotta pick it up."

She couldn't believe what she was hearing. "But Las Vegas is in *Nevada*, Jake!"

He had the audacity to look amused. "You make it sound like it's at the other end of the world. It's just over the state line."

Cordelia spoke through clenched teeth. "But we're supposed to be going to Yosemite. Remember? It was on the schedule."

"Oh, I remember the schedule, I just don't let it run my life." A smug look crept across his face. "Listen, we'll go to Yosemite tomorrow. You know, it's not even on the way to Eureka, and I didn't throw a fit about making a side trip there. Don't you think I deserve the same courtesy?"

Courtesy? Jake, the rudest boy in the Golden State, was asking *her* for some courtesy? She was trying hard not to freak out, but then heard another annoying rendition of "Jazzy Belle."

"Would you turn that damn thing off? I can't stand it anymore. It's making me crazy!" Her voice was so high and shrill that she might have punctured her own eardrums. Immediately afterward, Jake stifled a laugh, and Cordelia regretted showing him that he'd gotten under her skin.

He clicked something on the phone to silence it. "Here's the deal," he said. "I'll shut it off if you'll stop complaining all the rest of the way to Eureka."

There was a moment of silence.

"I'm not complaining," Cordelia said. "I'm just very vocal about my opinions."

"Fine, then no more phone, no more opinions. Cool?" Jake took his right hand off the steering wheel and extended it to Cordelia. She reached out slowly and then quickly shook it.

"How far is it to Las Vegas?" she asked.

His eyes narrowed.

"That's not a complaint, or even an opinion. It's a question," she pointed out.

"We'll be there in an hour," he said. "By the way, I bought you some lunch. It's in the bag in between the seats."

"Thanks." She tried not to sound too grateful, considering it would probably consist of two packets of beef jerky and an orange-flavor Gatorade. But when she opened the paper bag, what was inside was *soooooo* much better than that. She didn't even need to see the contents. She just smelled the familiar spicy goodness of Taco Bell beef burritos and practically melted into hot sauce.

She reached in and felt her hand wrap around the greasy paper-covered delights. The grease was seeping through a little and coating her hand, which felt so good, she almost cried. She had missed the Bell as much as she had missed the beach this week. In fact, now that she was thinking about it, she might have missed both of those things even more than she missed…

"Dig in, Cordy. I know you love to scarf down those double-decker tacos," Jake said.

"Uh…what are you talking about?"

"One night I dropped Molly off at your house, but I had to take a leak," he began.

Cordelia was anything but riveted.

"It was really late and you were in the kitchen hovering over this huge plate of tacos, and you were just going to town on them."

All of a sudden, this moment became crystal clear in her mind. Alexis had accidentally blurted out to Sam Cosmello that Cordelia had a crush on him and he'd written about it on his blog, which the entire school had read. She had been binge-eating out of depression and Jake had seen the whole thing! And now he was rubbing it in her face? How demented was that?

"Jake, let me ask you something."

"Go ahead," he replied.

"Why do you feel the need to embarrass me with a comment like that? Do you like putting me down? Does that make you feel better about yourself or something?"

When Jake turned to look at her briefly, Cordelia was very surprised by the upset expression that was on his face.

"Uh, no. I just thought you really liked Taco Bell so I picked some up for you. The End."

Weird. No witty retort? No mean-spirited comeback?

"I doubt that. What you said just made me feel really self-conscious, like I'm a fat pig or something."

Jake bristled. "Cordy, *you're* the one who jumped to that conclusion. All I said is that you must love tacos because you ate a whole plate of them one night."

Cordelia started to respond and then realized she had no idea what to say next. It was quite possible that Jacob Stein had just stumped her with one of his seemingly pointless observations. Only this time, what he'd said kind of made sense.

"Want to know what I think?"

She just glared at him.

"I think you have a hearing problem," he added. "You only hear what you want to hear, regardless of what someone is actually saying to you."

She couldn't listen to any more of this, and believe it

or not, she had completely lost her appetite. Jake didn't have the slightest idea what he was talking about. She heard him just fine, and what he always seemed to be saying was, "I'm better than you are." Plain and simple.

"Well, maybe if you watched your superior, high-and-mighty tone and how you phrase certain things, people wouldn't think that you're making fun of them."

At that, Jake muttered something and turned up Pedro the Lion so loud, a huge biker on a Harley yelled, "Turn that girlie crap down!"

The peaceful sensation that Cordelia felt yesterday came over her the second that Jake turned down the radio and the knob broke off in his hand. But this time, she didn't feel so great about finding her center again. Cordelia had a vision of Paul hearing what she'd just said and shaking his head in disappointment. Actually, she was not feeling so thrilled about herself either. Here she was, berating Jake for acting like he was better than everyone else, and the only way she could seem to find some serenity was to rejoice in Jake's misery. It was pretty apparent that the guy her older sister thought was a total "sweetie" just brought out the worst in her.

Cordelia felt the dry Nevada air seeping in through the crack in the window. She put her head in her hands and hoped that once she got to Yosemite and hugged Paul, everything would suddenly be fine.

Chapter Six

Cordelia felt rejuvenated as Jake drove the Charger through the Mojave Desert. Although it was very industrial along the highway, there were also some really scenic spots that were filled with sprawling shrubs and Joshua trees. Patches of unusually shaped cacti were scattered around the area, and there were exit signs directing travelers to various canyons, dunes, and mountain regions. Just the thought of these natural wonders reminded Cordelia how close she was to seeing Paul again. In a matter of hours (less than twenty-four, to be exact), they'd be laughing, talking, kissing, hugging, and almost, but not quite, having sex.

Ugh, back to that memory again, she thought.

Cordelia was still reeling a bit from the camping trip

and how she'd freaked the moment Paul wanted to take their hip-grinding festivities to a place where she had never gone before. She couldn't believe that she'd chickened out on him. She had to be certifiably insane.

She looked over to Jake, who was intermittently biting his fingernails and sipping on a Yoo-hoo. This had never really occurred to her before now, but had Jake and Molly had sex? And this would have been *before* he turned mega-hot. *Whoa.* That really shook Cordelia up. Jake had most likely kissed her sister all over her limber, ex-gymnast body, and Molly could have…

Oh God, Cordelia thought as a wave of nausea overcame her. She hunched over and put her head between her knees.

"Motion sickness?" Jake asked.

"That's one way to describe it," she replied.

"Want me to pull over?"

Cordelia felt a gnawing sensation grapple with either her large or small intestine (she couldn't tell which). "Yeah, thanks."

Jake veered off the nearest exit ramp, then pointed at a sign in excitement. "Hey, we're in Baker. The world's tallest outdoor thermometer is here!"

She rolled her eyes. "That's…impressive."

"You're right. I'm sure it's not close to anything you might see in, let's say, Yosemite," he teased.

"It's a big thermometer, Jake. How great can it be?"

"Why don't we check it out and see? You never know, it could rock your world."

"Doubtful," Cordelia mumbled as she massaged her stomach.

"Was that a complaint?"

She shot up. "No, definitely not."

"I think it was."

"Actually, it was more like—"

"An opinion? I thought we'd outlawed those, too," he interrupted. "You know what that means."

She sighed heavily as Jake turned his cell phone back on. Seconds afterward, "Jazzy Belle" began to sound once again.

"What can I say? I'm in demand," he said arrogantly before picking up the phone.

Cordelia groaned as they pulled in front of the Bun Boy complex, where the giant thermometer sat. As soon as they came to a stop, she opened the car door and leaned over, expecting to hurl. But then she realized that she had nothing to throw up. Jake had eaten everything in the Taco Bell bag, and when he'd stopped for gas a while ago, all she'd had was a few sticks of Trident.

Jake got out of the car and stretched while chatting on the phone. Cordelia could hear his conversation as she dangled out of the Charger and into the parking lot. He sounded as if he were being really nice. No caveman grunts or anything.

"Yep, I'm standing next to the big thermometer. You'd really get a kick out of this," she heard him say. "Of course, I wish you were here with me. Who else would get that this is the coolest thing ever?"

Her ears perked up. He surely wasn't talking to one of his buddies.

"Describe it to you? Well, it's like over one hundred feet tall and all these goofy tourists are taking pictures with it," Jake said through some laughter. "I know. I was thinking the exact same thing."

Cordelia got up out of her crouch and wandered over toward Jake. She stared at the big thermometer just as he did. The only thing she got from the experience was that it was currently ninety-four degrees out, which she could've guessed based on the way her ivory, SPF-15-covered skin was sizzling under the intense blaze of the California sun. Otherwise, it was completely, utterly uninteresting to her. Even less interesting than the red-legged honey-bird that Paul kept going on about.

Still, Jake kept laughing with whomever he was on the phone with, so apparently they thought this thing was a regular hoot. She gazed at it from different angles. That didn't help either. And the more Jake giggled and guffawed, the more self-conscious Cordelia felt. She was flirting with the notion that her nemesis may be right—what if she was wound way too tightly to enjoy the hilarity of this—or anything, for that matter?

"Okay, well, I gotta go. Your sister looked like she was going to puke, so I'd better get her to a handicapped restroom quick," he said into the phone.

What the hell?

Jake clicked off his cell and put it in his pocket. "Molly says hi."

Cordelia gasped. "You were talking to Molly this whole time?"

He shrugged. "Yeah. So?"

"She didn't say she wanted to speak to me?"

"Um, no. What's the problem?"

Cordelia felt her eyelids twitching uncontrollably. "I better get some crackers and ginger ale," she said as she made her way toward the nearby country store.

"Grab me another Yoo-hoo!" Jake shouted.

She was about to turn around, scream "Yoo-hoo this!" and give him the finger, but she didn't. Cordelia was just too rattled by what had happened. Jake still seemed to be into her sister, and even worse, from the way he was acting, it seemed as if he believed Molly was the only person who would ever truly understand him.

And that's when it hit her. Why she hadn't slept with Paul that day. Even though he was great and nice and gorgeous and smart, the one thing that she needed to feel sure of deep down in her gut just wasn't quite there. Did she truly understand Paul, and as much as he seemed to like her, did he really understand her?

Maybe she'd find out in another twenty-three hours.

*   *   *

An hour and a half later, Cordelia, Jake, and the Charger rambled down Sunset Road in Las Vegas, where Jake's ex-roommate, Mike, lived in an off-campus apartment. She'd never been to Vegas before, but she'd seen enough films and TV shows to know what the Strip was like. There'd be flashing neon signs towering above all the out-of-towners and gamblers who were trying their luck at the casinos. There'd be all-night restaurants, cabaret bars featuring topless dancers, and drunk people who were attending bachelor or bachelorette parties.

That kind of thing wasn't necessarily Cordelia's idea of a good time. She'd much rather be listening to the roar of the waves at Pacific Beach and watching the sunset while lying down on a fluffy blanket. But she could see why people might get swept up in the glitziness of the city. They were only a few blocks from the Strip and she could feel the giddy vibe of people who were about to embark on an evening of debauchery.

As for Cordelia, she would be spending another action-packed evening in Jacob Stein hell.

"This must be the place," he said, and swerved into a

parking lot facing a row of apartments. A sign greeted them: WELCOME TO PARADISE COVE.

The complex was actually pretty nice. Cordelia liked the beach-inspired style of the place and the open, airy architecture. Some of the windows held flower boxes, and pansies lined the walkway leading up to Mike's unit. All of it reminded her of home.

"There it is. Apartment twelve," Jake said.

But before they could get out, a large husky guy wearing a stained fraternity T-shirt, ripped cutoff jean shorts, and a backward UNLV baseball cap came bumbling out. "Yo, bro!" he yelled.

Jake jumped out of the car while the other guy leaped over the ledge and enveloped him in a bear hug.

Then the friendly stranger came around to the side and opened her door. She got out and took a good look at him. Red hair, bright blue eyes, freckles all over his nose and cheeks, and the goofiest, sweetest smile she'd seen on any boy.

"Hey, you must be Cordy. I'm Mike Cavanaugh."

Cordelia immediately felt relaxed around Mike. He was that likable off the bat. "Nice to meet you," she said, shaking his hand.

"Your stuff in the trunk?" Mike asked.

"We'll get it later," Jake said. "I'm wiped out and starving."

Mike chuckled. "You're tired? Please, dude. How

many all-nighters did you pull cramming for tests? Cordy, this guy was a total geek last semester. Barely partied at all."

She eyed Jake, who seemed to already regret introducing her to Mike. "Is that so?"

"Oh my God. The guy never stopped studying. I thought his head was going to explode."

Jake put his hands in his pockets and slumped over a bit as if he'd been humiliated. Cordelia just smiled. All this time she'd thought Jake was a slacker, but apparently behind closed doors he was a hard worker. How crazy was that?

Mike ushered them into his apartment, which was in typical college-guy condition. Beer cans were strewn around the living room; the kitchen was covered in empty pizza boxes; and there was a scent in the air that reminded Cordelia of either kitty litter or maximum strength kitty litter.

"Maid's day off," Mike said with a grin. He opened a pizza box that had TONY'S emblazoned on the top and held out a cold slice to Cordy. "Want a snack? If you don't like this, I've got plenty of stuff in the pantry."

"You've got a pantry?" Jake asked.

"Yeah," Mike said. "Most people call it a coat closet, but whatever. There is a ton of food in there. Doritos, Combos, pretty much anything ending with 'os.'"

Cordelia laughed. "Bring on the Doritos."

"Salsa, Cooler Ranch, or Guacamole flavored?"

"Cooler Ranch," Cordelia and Jake said in unison.

"Aw, how sweet," Mike said while punching Jake in the arm. "You guys are like twins or something."

"Just get the chips," Jake snarled.

Mike disappeared into the other room.

Cordelia couldn't help but smirk at Jake.

"What?" he said, irritated.

"I'm just happy we agree on something," she replied.

"Don't get too happy. It's probably a sign of the end of the world."

Cordelia put her hands on her hips. "And how come you never told me you were a nerd?"

"I didn't know you were so interested," Jake said, raising an eyebrow.

"I'm not," she said quickly.

It was strange, though. She kind of was interested.

Mike came back with three bags of Cooler Ranch Doritos. "One for each of us," he announced.

Jake patted Mike on the back with brute force. "Thanks, man. You're a gracious host."

"So, what do you guys want to do tonight?" Mike asked.

"How about you and me heading out to a casino?" Jake suggested.

That pissed Cordelia off. Jake obviously didn't want

her to tag along. What, wasn't she cool enough to go? She could certainly hold her own with these guys.

Mike nodded. "Sounds good to me." He turned to Cordelia. "How about you? Wanna tear up the Strip?"

"She can't go," Jake snapped. "Cordy can't pass for twenty-one like us."

"That's ridiculous," Cordelia said.

"Doesn't even matter," Mike said flippantly. "I'm tight with one of the bouncers at Mandalay Bay; he'll let her in."

Jake fidgeted. "Well, gambling's not her thing anyway. She's more of the stay-at-home-and-knit type."

"You are so full of crap, Jake," she said curtly.

Mike let out a belly laugh. "Seems like she's feisty to me, man. I say she's in."

Cordelia wasn't usually a gloater, but she just couldn't help herself this time. She took a chip, tossed it into her mouth, and then gave Jake her best "so there" grin.

Judging from what she knew of Mike, she had a good feeling that she might even have fun tonight. Now if only Molly were around to help her pick out what to wear....

Chapter Seven

Cordelia arrived at Mandalay Bay around ten thirty that night. She was dressed in her very, *very* skimpy purple dress and flanked by two really good-looking guys. This could mean only one thing. They had all somehow traveled into some alternate Molly-engineered universe, where everybody was gorgeous and destined to have a good time.

In fact, Cordelia had been feeling rather Mollyesque ever since she'd left Paradise Cove. She had called her sister to ask what kind of ensemble would make her look older, but all she got was voice mail: "Leave a message for Molly. Ciao!" So Cordelia had had to fend for herself. Luckily, she was in possession of Molly's suitcase, which was filled with clothes her sister called ARAP (As

Revealing As Possible) and an unlimited supply of fruit-scented beauty products.

She wasn't able to find anything that fit her, though—Molly's torso was very long and lean while the distance between Cordelia's neck and waist measured exactly fifteen inches. (She calculated these types of things very carefully.) But she'd remembered that she'd agreed to pack that sexy get-up Molly had given her for her birthday. After applying a light coat of Cargo bronzer on her sun-deprived face and Tarte glistening powder on her arms and legs, she'd slipped the dress on, thrown on her favorite strappy Steve Madden platform sandals (for maximum height), and pinned her hair up in a loose French twist.

From the way Mike kept checking her out and flirting with her on the ride over, and the unblinking stare the bouncer was giving her that very minute, Cordelia realized that it was the first time she actually resembled her sister. Wherever she turned, boys' mouths were agape. She may have even spotted a little bit of drooling.

But there was absolutely, positively no reaction from Jacob Stein. Not even a "You look nice," or a "Cool shoes." In fact, when Mike had opened his car door for her earlier, Jake pushed right past her, yelled "Shotgun," and then jumped into the passenger seat. Her juiced-up appearance had not affected him at all, not that Cordelia cared or anything.

Mike punched his bouncer friend playfully on the shoulder. "How's it hanging, big guy?"

"Things are cool, man," he replied. "Are these friends of yours?"

"Yeah, this is Jake. He was my roommate last year," Mike said as he peered into a window and checked out how his hair gel was holding up. In a pair of tight-fitting sandblasted Lucky jeans and a navy blue button-down shirt, Mike cleaned up real good (as opposed to Jake, who didn't even change his sweaty I-want-you-to-think-I-got-this-at-a-thrift-shop-but-I-really-bought-it-at-Aéropostale T-shirt).

Jake shook the bouncer's hand firmly. "Hey."

"And who is this fine young thing?" the bouncer asked.

An enormous lump formed in Cordelia's throat. She'd never had an older guy leer at her like this before, and it was making her uncomfortable. Then Mike put his arm around her and pulled her close, which made her feel a bit more protected.

"Cordy's with me," he replied. "She's a sophomore at University of South Carolina. We met on the Internet. Isn't that right, sweetie?"

At first, Cordelia was totally confused. But quickly she realized that Mike was just trying to help her get into the casino, so she thought she should play along. "That's right, honey."

Mike kissed her on the forehead and winked at the bouncer. "She's the one; I can feel it."

Suddenly, Jake coughed something under his breath, which sounded kind of like, "Shutthehellup."

The bouncer threw back his head and laughed. "Get your ass inside before somebody else spots ya."

"Thanks," Mike said, pushing Cordelia and Jake ahead of him.

As soon as Cordelia went through the revolving door, she couldn't believe her eyes. Mandalay Bay was like nothing she'd ever seen before. She kind of expected to be blinded by gaudiness, but the place was actually very classy. Well-dressed and distinguished-looking people were milling about. In the center of the room, there was a gigantic island, filled with foliage, palm trees, and cascading water, underneath a ceiling painted like the desert sky. A golden glow emanated from above them and covered the room in a dizzying haze. The game tables were made out of dark oak, and the dealers wore crisp uniforms and appeared to be in control with each flip of the card.

When the group came to a halt in the middle of the casino floor, Jake shoved Mike really hard. Cordelia flinched. She wasn't sure if he was just fooling around or not, but Jake seemed rather aggravated.

"What was that for?"

"For being a shit. We almost got busted back there," Jake replied.

"I told you, me and Rudy are buds," Mike said stiffly. "Relax, dude. Why do you have to be so high-strung?"

Cordelia couldn't contain her laughter. "Bawah-ha-ha!"

Jake turned and sneered at her. "What's so funny?"

She glared right back. "Nothing."

Jake thrust his hands into his pockets and gazed over at the craps tables. Meanwhile, Mike seemed to be over their spat already. He eyed one of the many young women in micro miniskirts and sequined asymmetrical tank tops who were moving through the crowds, holding trays of paper umbrella-embellished cocktails.

"Want something to drink?" Mike asked her.

"Just a Diet Coke or something like that," Cordelia replied. "Thanks."

Mike nodded approvingly. "Smart," he said. "You know why they push the free drinks at these places, don't you? So people will get tanked and blow more money."

Cordelia could see that. People were either blitzed and stumbling around, looking very happy and screaming things like, "One more mai tai!" or zonked out in front of slot machines, their bodies operating on automatic as they rhythmically shoved tokens into slots and pulled levers.

A Brooke Burke clone showed up and handed Cordelia a soda.

"Jack on the rocks?" she said to Mike, who slipped her a small wad of cash in exchange for her phone number.

Cordelia watched Jake's reaction. He rolled his eyes and huffed as if he was annoyed at Mike for acting like a slick gambler. This really surprised her. Why would it matter to Jake what Mike did? He was as laid-back as they come, right? Nothing ever fazed him and everything was a big joke. He loved pointing out how Cordelia's organized and structured nature was a complete buzzkill. Now here they were in an amazing Las Vegas casino and Jake seemed just so…cautious.

"All right, lady and gentleman. We've got money to burn and liquor to ingest," Mike said right before throwing back his entire glass of Jack Daniel's.

Jake frowned. "Take it easy, man. It's early."

"There aren't any clocks in here for a reason, dude. So we won't know what time it is."

"You're a risk-taker, Jake. Don't *you* want to gamble?" Cordelia asked sarcastically.

"Of course, he does. Let's start playing and win big. I'm in the mood for a steak tonight." Mike put his empty glass on a waitress's tray and ordered another JD. Then he turned to Cordelia. "Okay, what's your game?"

"Cordy doesn't have a game," Jake said. "She's not into fun."

She shot him a venomous look. *Just ignore him and maybe he'll evaporate into thin air,* she thought.

"So what's good for a beginner? The slot machines?"

"Nah, slots are for suckers," Mike said. "Try roulette."

But before they could begin, they all had to pay a visit to the cashier booths.

"How much do you want to spend, high roller?" Mike asked with a grin.

Cordelia pulled out some money from her wallet. "Ten dollars' worth, please," she told the woman at the window.

"That's not going to get you anywhere," Mike advised. "You gotta spend money to make money."

Jake had to add his two cents, of course. "Don't buy any more chips, Cordy. I'm serious. You can't risk more than you're willing to lose. That's how you get into trouble."

There was this fatherly tone in his voice that sounded so condescending, and Cordelia was tired of hearing it. What were the odds that Jake had ever said something like that to Molly? Slim to none. If Molly had put down a million dollars, Jake probably would have told her how savvy and reckless and cool she was being. If Molly had put down a nickel, Jake probably would have commented on how wise and smart she was being. Cordelia was facing the facts. Jake criticized her every move, but he never did that to Molly, no matter how frivolous or careless she was. Which is precisely why Cordelia took out all the money in her wallet and slapped it down in front of the cashier.

"Are you nuts?" Jake exclaimed.

"That's ballsy, girl," Mike said. "I like your style." He grabbed a fresh drink and led them to a table where hopeful gamblers were placing chips on a board of red and black numbered squares.

"What's your lucky number?" Mike asked.

"I don't have one," Cordelia said. "No, wait, I'll play my age."

"Shh!" Mike hissed. "Don't let the dealer hear you!"

Cordelia giggled. Her hand had been hovering over sixteen, but she moved it swiftly to twenty-one red, and she placed a chip on it. A man in a gold-braid uniform spun a wheel and then tossed in the marble. "Twenty-one red!" he yelled.

She let out a squeal and clapped her hands. How easy was that? The dealer tossed another token her way. Cordelia took both and put them on fifteen red. The wheel was spun, the marble was dropped; and—"Fifteen red!"

"Hey, you're on a roll!" Mike shouted.

Jake tapped Cordelia hard on the shoulder and she spun around.

"What?" she growled.

"Quit now while you're ahead."

"Jake, she's hot. Why are you trying to spoil it?" Mike said.

Cordelia smiled at Jake when she saw him get annoyed. "I'm gonna let it ride," she said cheerfully.

"Suit yourself," Jake muttered. "Now *I* need a drink."

Strangely enough, he up and vanished into the crowd, just as Cordelia had hoped he would. Now that she had experienced a little of her own Vegas magic, she figured she might as well see where it would take her, and the farther away from Jake she went, the better.

"Your turn to pick a number," she said to Mike.

"You could start spreading the chips around," he suggested. "That gives you better odds."

So she did. She tried different combinations—the digits that made up her phone number, her social security number, and the day that Mike's dog died. In every spin of the wheel, she got something. It was such a rush, especially because a crowd began to gather. Each time she won more chips, Mike would throw his arms around her and pick her up off the floor. When she got up to the three-hundred-dollar mark, he began twirling her like a ballet dancer and dipping her. She wasn't sure if he was excited because she was on a streak or because he had finished his fifth Jack on the rocks. Either way, it was so much fun to be with someone who was cheering her on. In fact, the entire room seemed to be clapping for her.

"You're beautiful," Mike said, grinning from ear to ear. "Keep it up!"

Cordelia felt like she was floating. She was so giddy, her stomach was fluttering with anticipation. She looked across the table at another player, who just took in a fortune on the last spin. She realized she could make a lot more if she bet more than one chip on a number. So during the next round, she tried two. But she lost.

"Don't worry about it," Mike said calmly. "Try it again."

Then she tried three and won. By the time she got to ten, people were shaking her hand, slapping her on the back, and one guy asked for a kiss. She blew one in his direction and laughed. This was completely wild!

All of sudden, her practical, common-sense inner voice began to sound off. "Quit now while you're ahead."

Wait a second, she wondered. *That's what Jake had said.*

The adrenaline in Cordelia's bloodstream was at an all-time high. She couldn't stop. She'd be a fool to cash in.

"Quit now while you're ahead."

God, shut up, shut up, SHUT UP! she thought.

Mike pulled her close to him, and Cordelia winced when she smelled his sour breath. "You know, if *yoush* put all those *chipsh* on a winning number, you'd have over a *thoushandth* dollars," he slurred.

A thousand dollars? The image of a shopping spree at Hold Everything danced in her head. So did the image of Paul opening up a gift box containing a pair of state-of-the-art binoculars and her mom unwrapping a new Williams-Sonoma cooking set.

She didn't analyze her decision any further than that

and pushed all the chips onto one square. The dealer spun the wheel. The marble rolled around for what seemed like weeks. Cordelia grabbed Mike's hand and squeezed it hard. The marble bounced around, hitting off numbers left and right. She was sweating and twitching and laughing like a mad scientist. And then...

Cordelia went cold as the casino worker made her mountain of chips disappear as quickly as Jake had about an hour ago.

"Oh boy," Mike whimpered. "You lost."

She dug down deep and did everything in her power not to faint. "I didn't just lose. I lost *everything*."

Up until this point, the biggest shock of Cordelia's life had been when Alexis Dunbar won the presidency by five votes in their eighth-grade election. That was nothing compared to this horror. Her money was gone forever and it was all her own fault.

She was hyperventilating as if she'd just taken off in a twin-engine plane. Mike had to flag another waitress down for some water.

"Just breathe in and out, Cordy," he said, sounding a lot like Paul would have had he been there to witness her humiliation.

But Cordelia knew that wasn't going to help. Nothing could possibly stop the wicked thoughts in her mind that were taunting her over and over again:

You should have listened to Jake.

Chapter Eight

Cordelia was still crouched down on the floor, trying to recover from what Mike was calling the Vegas Shitstorm, when she heard the following seven words.

"Guess who made a killing at blackjack."

She didn't want to look up and see who was talking to them, but she didn't have to. She could identify the sound of Jake's shrill, mocking voice from a hundred yards away. Still, Cordelia knew she'd have to get up off the ground eventually. This was as good a time as any.

Mike helped her up a little bit, but then let go prematurely when he caught a glimpse of the huge mound of money that Jake was holding in his hand. "Why, you crafty bastard!"

"That's me," Jake declared happily. "I just booked us a suite for tonight."

"Excellent." Mike hiccupped and then turned to Cordelia. "See? Things are looking up, buttercup."

Cordelia was in such a deranged mental state that she couldn't fully absorb any of their words. Her head still felt fuzzy and she couldn't stop her thoughts from racing ahead of her.

I'll have to call home and ask for money. Mom and Dad will want to know why. And then I'll have to tell them that I snuck into a casino, gambled even though I am underage, and lost every cent I had. They'll freak out like a couple of head cases and then tell me to come home. Damn! What would Molly do in a situation like this?

Cordelia stopped herself. She'd dressed up like Molly tonight and look where it had taken her—the Land of Big, Scary Trouble.

"Hey, Cordelia. Did you hear what I said?"

Jake was snapping his fingers in front of her face again. Cordelia grabbed his hand and clenched it tightly.

"I swear on the grave of…someone *really* important…next time you snap at me, I'll break your fingers."

Jake turned to Mike. "What's *her* problem?"

Mike let out a reverberating burp. "I told her to pick number eight, man, but she had to go with some girl named Alexis's address."

"Oh Christ," Jake said warily. "Cordelia, how much did you lose?"

"Dude, she's totaled," Mike said, pulling Cordelia into a tight bear hug. "And she's *sooooooo* sad!"

A waitress passed by with another tray of drinks, so Mike suddenly released Cordelia and sent her stumbling into Jake. When he grabbed onto her, she noticed how strong his grip was. When his sleeves shifted up a bit, she could see his biceps clenching. As she put her arms around his shoulders to brace herself, she was close enough to feel his breath on her cheek. Apparently Cordelia could be extremely detail-oriented and distraught at the exact same time.

Jake helped her find her balance and stand on her own two feet.

That was very chivalrous of him, she thought. *Why didn't he just drop me on my ass, like I know he's dying to?*

Then Jacob Stein showed his true colors once again. "I told you so!"

"Wow, I can't believe you held that in for ten seconds. What restraint!" she shouted.

"Don't get all upset with me. I told you not to get in over your head, but you were so hell-bent on being a big shot."

Cordelia could feel that her skin was burning hot. "You're such a hypocrite. Yesterday you said I was always playing it safe. And now that I took a risk, you're saying I should have done the opposite."

"I'm surprised that you're even listening to me at all. You act as if you don't have anything to learn from anyone," Jake said defiantly.

"And *you* don't act the same way?"

They were toe-to-toe when Mike came staggering back with a whole bottle of Absolut.

"I just told 'em to put this on my tab," he said slowly.

"But you don't have a tab," Cordelia reminded him.

"That's why I said my name was Jacob Stein."

Jake rolled his eyes. "Whatever. Let's just go up to the room."

She crossed her arms over her chest and followed behind them silently. She had no other choice. Jake was the one with rivers of cash coming out of his ears, and all she had was the teeny-tiny purple dress on her back. Like it or not, she was at his mercy.

*   *   *

Cordelia should have been happier than the time her parents took her to Gymboree on her fifth birthday party (it had been the highlight of her year). A luxury suite in the Mandalay Bay hotel was like an adult version of Gymboree—there were plasma cable TVs in every room (including a small one in front of the toilet) and a huge sitting area with enormous plushy couches and a fully stocked minibar. The two adjoining bedrooms had gigantic king-size, four-poster beds that were covered in thick layers of soft, silky comforters, shams, and pillowcases. The place was polished and decadent from the bottom of the thick colorful rugs to the top of the high ceilings.

It was way beyond Cordelia's high lodging standards and Travelocity's definition of five-star accommodations. But there was absolutely no way she could enjoy any of it, because she had to share this hotel paradise with the vile, reprehensible Jacob Stein and his wasted sidekick, Mike "I ♥ reinforcing Irish stereotypes" Cavanaugh.

She was sitting on the love seat, counting the many ways in which she had derailed her summer by agreeing to this trip with Jake, when Mike plopped down next to her and spilled some vodka on the upholstery. Jake had run out to the car to pick up his backpack and Cordelia's overnight bag, so she was put on watch-Mike-and-make-sure-he-doesn't-break-anything duty (oh joy of joys).

"So, Cordy," Mike said while slurping his beverage. "What do you think of our digs? Pretty nice, huh?"

She simply nodded her head in affirmation. After the evening she'd had, the last thing she wanted to do was get into a conversation with someone who'd had more to drink in one night than most people do in a week.

"Are you still upset about what happened at the casino yesterday?" he asked.

"Mike, that happened an hour ago," Cordelia corrected.

He scratched his head before scratching someplace else that was highly inappropriate. "Whatever. It's in the past. Forget about it."

"I can't. I don't have any more money, and if I call home and tell my parents, they'll be really pissed off," she explained.

Suddenly, she felt something clammy and moist land on her right knee. That thing was Mike's hand.

Oh God, she thought. *This can't be happening.*

"Don't worry, I've got you covered," he said, leaning in closer.

Cordelia couldn't believe this. Mike was actually making a move on her! She had no idea what to do. He was Jake's good friend and obviously he wasn't using any of his remaining brain cells. She didn't want to offend him by saying or doing anything too rash.

Wait, I should mention Paul. That will stop him in his tracks.

"Actually, I think if I call my boyfriend, he'll be able to help me out. Thanks, though. That's really sweet of you to offer," she replied.

But he didn't seem like he was backing off. In fact, she thought she saw his eyebrows go up, as if things had just gotten more interesting.

"Well, your boyfriend isn't here, you know."

Mike's hand was moving slowly up her thigh.

Cordelia's heart was palpitating so hard she swore all of Las Vegas could feel the shock waves. She was going to freak out any minute now; she could feel it. The more he inched toward her and the more she tried to crawl away from him, the more she could sense that her knee was centimeters away from his very vulnerable area.

She remembered how Molly used to tell her when they were kids that if any creepy guys ever tried to hurt her, she had to kick them where it counted. Then she'd demonstrate the maneuver on a male Cabbage Patch Kid. The way this situation was going, it seemed as if it might be one of the few times she'd ever have to follow any of Molly's advice.

"Listen, I think you need to go sleep this off," she said sternly. "I mean it, Mike. You're drunk."

"And you're absolutely lovely," he said seductively, and went in for a kiss.

Cordelia had no choice.

Hello, Mike's crotch. I'd like to introduce you to my knee.

Jake entered the room as soon as Mike had crumpled like a house of cards.

"What the hell is going on?" he shouted, and dropped their bags.

At that moment, Cordelia had never been happier to see him. She rushed over and gave him a hug while Mike writhed on the ground in pain.

"Are you okay?" Jake asked him.

Mike was only capable of grunting sounds that were incomprehensible.

"I'm so sorry, but he was trying to kiss me and I had to fend him off."

Cordelia watched Jake's face crinkle up and turn a rare shade of purple. Sweat was beading off his forehead, and his neck was getting very blotchy and irritated. She knew what this meant. After all, she had just busted his best friend's balls. Her eyes scanned the room, looking for places to run for cover.

But before she could crouch down under the executive maple wood desk, Jake crossed the room and pulled Mike up by his shirt collar.

"I can't believe what an asshole you are!" he yelled. "You had no right doing that to Cordy."

Mike didn't do much but whimper something that sounded like an apology. But Jake wouldn't listen.

"Go to bed and stay there," he said while dragging Mike into one of the bedrooms.

Once they were out of sight, Cordelia could hear the two of them arguing. Mike tried to defend himself a little and then asked for forgiveness. Yet Jake was really hard on him. He said that he was sick of bailing Mike out of trouble and that's why he'd had to leave UNLV in the first place. He just couldn't take that kind of pressure. Jake also told Mike that Cordelia was not just some girl he could fool around with, that she was a good person who didn't deserve to be put in that position. Then his voice dropped lower and Cordelia couldn't make out what he was saying.

When Jake reentered the lounge area, Cordelia could see that he was still very upset.

"Is everything okay?" she asked.

Jake rubbed the back of his neck. "That's what I should be asking you."

"I'm fine."

"Too bad Mike can't say the same for himself," he said with a chuckle. "You worked him over really good."

Cordelia giggled. "It's a little trick that Molly taught me."

He smirked. "Well, I'm glad you never used it on me."

"You were asking for it, though. Plenty of times."

"Thankfully you are better at restraining yourself than I am."

She saw something really warm in his eyes just then, but it went just as quickly as it came.

"So, are you hungry?" he asked abruptly. "We could order some room service. I've got to make sure Mike drinks ten liters of water and doesn't choke on his vomit, so I'll be up all night."

"Sounds like a blast," she replied.

"Unfortunately, I'm used to it." Jake picked up the room phone and began to dial. "So what'll it be? I'm sure they have everything here."

Cordelia frowned. "I'll just have some of Mike's water."

He gave her a sideways glance. "This isn't prison, Cordy. You can have whatever you want."

"But I'm broke, remember?"

"Listen, you can enter all your expenses into your Treo and add them up later. Then mail me a check or something. I know you're good for it," he said.

"Really?"

She was so taken aback by how nice he was being, she wasn't sure how to react.

"Yes, now order some food before I change my mind," Jake added.

Cordelia smiled. "How about a nice heaping plate of tacos?"

He smiled in return. "Make that two of 'em."

＊　　＊　　＊

Twenty minutes later, Jake and Cordelia had something between a Thanksgiving feast and an impromptu picnic spread out all over the bed. In addition to the tacos, they ordered lobster bisque, a Waldorf salad, garlic mashed potatoes, creamed corn, and two pieces of chocolate blackout cake. The remnants of their meal were scattered around them while they both reclined on a mound of cushions and rubbed their bellies.

"I think my intestines are going to collapse," Cordelia said as she licked a stray piece of icing off her spoon.

Jake took off the napkin he'd clipped to his T-shirt and waved it in the air in surrender. "Mine already did. You may have to pump my stomach."

"Why did you make me eat so much?" She brought her knees up to her chest.

"You didn't need any encouragement from me, Cordy. I wasn't the one who inhaled the cake."

Cordelia swatted him playfully on the shoulder and he laughed. Then something really curious happened. For a second, she thought she was imagining it, but then it happened again. Jake was definitely, without a doubt, checking out her legs. At first, he just quickly looked over. Then the next time it was a lingering glance.

"I'm going to check on Mike again. Be right back," he said hurriedly before darting out of the room.

She was so startled by it that the moment he took off, she dove into her bag and changed into her Hollister sweatpants and an oversized T-shirt. Even after that, Cordelia felt spooked. This was Jacob Stein. King of the Pains in the Ass. Molly's ex-boyfriend. Guy who repulsed her since the day they'd laid eyes on each other.

What really spooked her, though, was that she kind of liked the fact that Jake had his eyes on her. In fact, it was difficult for her to admit to herself how exhilarated she felt. It was so odd. A little while ago she was fending off someone's advances by invoking the name of her boyfriend and kneeing him in the family jewels, and here she was, intrigued by the fact that her adversary had shown some interest in her.

This is complete insanity, she said to herself. *I'm seeing Paul tomorrow and I'm beginning to think that I need my head examined before I do.*

Jake came back into the room and began cleaning up. He was more fidgety now than when he'd left, as if he were nervous or preoccupied.

Cordelia joined in. "So is Mike feeling any better?"

"Yeah, he just drank another two glasses of water and zonked out again."

"That's good," she said.

"I really hope he shapes up, you know? He's got a good head on his shoulders when he's not trying to give himself alcohol poisoning."

She gazed at Jake as he put their dishes onto the large room service trays. He seemed more mature all of a sudden. "He's lucky to have you as a friend."

"Yeah, well," he said with a quizzical look on his face. "This friend needs to unwind."

Suddenly Jake reached over to the night table, where he had put his drumsticks. He took them and tapped out a rhythm on all the plates and glasses on the tray. It was quick and snappy, like something she'd heard on her father's jazz records. Cordelia kept her eyes on his hands as they danced and twirled the sticks around. She couldn't believe what she was seeing and hearing. It was incredible, fantastic, and coming from the mind of Jacob Stein.

When he was finished, he threw one of his sticks into the air and caught it in his hand. Cordelia could do nothing but applaud, and Jake even blushed a little bit.

"Wow," she said. "Jake, you really—"

"Suck?" he interrupted.

"Shut up! I was going to say it was very good."

"I was just riffing."

Cordelia shook her head. "Well, whatever it was, it sounded amazing."

Jake's face lit up. "Thanks, Cordy."

"No problem," she said, turning her gaze to the floor.

"If I'm any good at it, it's because I think it's really fun," he added. "Want to hear something weird?"

She looked back up at him and grinned. "Sure."

"You didn't check your Treo once tonight, or freak out at Mike's because he lived in a germ-infested pit. You looked incredible, snuck into a casino, gambled away all of your money, kneed a man in the testicles, and stuffed yourself full of fattening food. And the weird thing is, I have a feeling that you had more than your fair share of fun. Didn't you?"

Cordelia just stared at him. She was utterly speechless.

"I thought so." Jake picked up the tray full of dishes and walked toward the door. Then he paused and turned around to say one last thing. "I'm sleeping on the floor in Mike's room tonight, so the bed's all yours. See ya in the morning."

"Yeah, see ya," she said softly as he ambled away.

Then she sat down on the mattress to steady herself and let what Jake had said sink in. It was all true, every last word of it. But Cordelia was fixated on one particular thing that he'd said.

"You looked incredible."

Chapter Nine

Cordelia checked her Swatch. Three P.M. On an ordinary Thursday, she would be losing her mind because she was behind schedule, but today, she just felt like coasting. It all started with the morning. Everyone crawled out of bed around noon—no alarms, no wake-up calls. They just got up when they felt like it. (Cordelia hadn't done that since her last sleepover two years ago and had forgotten how great it was.) Mike had been the last one to slink out of his room. He'd looked like an eighteen-wheeler had parked on top of him for the night, but at least he'd had the decency to beg Cordelia for her forgiveness, which she gave without hesitation. Everything seemed to be back to normal when they dropped Mike off at his apartment. It was after two when they'd hit the road, and Jake was still at the wheel of the Charger, chugging along at speeds that would even agitate elderly drivers.

She'd called Paul once they'd departed to let him know what time they'd be arriving. She'd calculated the distance on her Treo and double-checked it online. Yet once they entered the depths of Death Valley, she was a little worried that they might never make it. At first glance, it seemed as if they were in the capital of Desolationville, population zero. The area had this eerie quality that made it both beautiful and ominous at the same time.

But as they kept going, Cordelia's concern began to drift off into the cirrus clouds that were scattered in the crisp indigo sky. They drove by mountain ranges—the gigantic size of them made Cordelia feel really small and insignificant and even a bit lost. Then the car made its way through long stretches of road that were surrounded by either the sandy, golden desert or jagged rock formations that spread out across the canyons. There were natural gorges and huge craters that might have been created by volcanic activity many, many years ago. Every time they turned a corner, some unique piece of breathtaking scenery was just waiting to befall Cordelia's eyes. She couldn't predict what was on the horizon or make everything fit into some perfect organized structure or overanalyze any of it. For once in her life, that was okay. In fact, it was more than okay. It was unbelievably great.

Too bad the Charger had to ruin it all.

"Do you hear that?" Jake asked suddenly.

"What?"

"Funny noises. Coming from the engine."

Cordelia listened. There was a clanking sound she hadn't noticed before. "Is that bad?"

"Well, it's certainly not good." He leaned over the wheel and peered into the distance. "I think that's a rest stop off this service road up ahead. Hope we can make it."

So did Cordelia. Breaking down in a place called Death Valley was anything but appealing. The glare on the windshield was particularly strong, so the last thing they needed was to be stuck out in the intense heat.

The clanking was getting really loud by the time the car pulled up in front of what Jake had thought was a rest stop. Unfortunately, upon closer inspection, the building seemed abandoned, and there wasn't another car in sight.

Then Cordelia heard the worst sound of all—there was only absolute silence after the Charger sputtered to a complete halt.

Jake exhaled loudly. "Shit."

He stomped on the accelerator and tried to start the engine again. But nothing happened. He did it several more times in a row, but that didn't help either.

"You don't want to flood it," Cordelia warned him.

There was a flicker of annoyance in his eyes. "I've got this under control."

Figures he'd dismiss my advice, she thought.

Jake took out the keys from the ignition, put them back in, and tried to start the car once more. When there was no response, he pounded his fist against the wheel with all his might. "Goddamn it!"

Now Cordelia was really nervous. Jake was so anxious, she was certain he might turn psychotic. He got out of the car and slammed the door behind him. The air-conditioning had only been off for a couple of minutes and Cordelia was already sweltering. She followed Jake out of the Charger, hoping that would help cool her off. But it was even worse in the open because there were no trees to shield them from the scorching sun. The heat was going to her head quickly; she could barely think straight.

"We'll have to call for a tow." Jake wiped his brow with the bottom of his shirt and ran his hands through his dampening dark hair. "Good thing I didn't blow all my winnings from last night, because this is going to cost a ton. Do you have your phone on you?"

"Hold on, I'll get it." She reached back into the Charger and grabbed it from her bag. Meanwhile, Jake opened the hood of the car, but then just stood there and stared at it wistfully.

"It's probably something really simple," he said after a moment of contemplation.

"Like what?"

"Maybe the battery is run down and we just need someone with cables to give us a charge." He looked down the empty road and sighed.

"Well, in the meantime, I'll call information for a tow truck," Cordelia said. But when she tried to dial out on her Treo, she knew she wouldn't be making any calls for a while. "Holy Christ."

"What?"

"I forgot to recharge it last night!"

"That's okay," Jake said. "Given everything that went on, I'm not surprised."

"Well, I am. I never forget stuff like this. Never," Cordelia declared.

"Don't get all worked up, Cordy. My phone is in my backpack." Jake started toward the rear of the car.

She was starting to feel faint. "But how will we access any of the directions? Or the maps or the itineraries?"

"We'll just have to improvise." Jake fiddled with his key ring and popped the trunk.

Improvise? Cordelia was distracted by a welcoming noise. "Wait, someone's coming!" she cried out. Sure enough, a small truck was careening around the bend. "I'll flag him down!"

She heard Jake yell something, but she didn't

want to miss this chance at getting out of this mess. Besides, she was just improvising, like he'd said. She dashed to the side of the road, waved her arms wildly, and the truck slowed down. As it rolled to a stop, she flashed Jake a triumphant look as if she had saved the day.

Jake wasn't paying any attention to her. He was watching the man who came out of the truck.

"Howdy."

Cordelia turned to the skinny man in the grease-stained sleeveless T-shirt that read, WHO FARTED? She caught a whiff of his breath (which resembled Mike's from the night before), so she stepped back a bit to put some distance between them. "We're having car trouble. Do you think you could help us?"

The man strode past her and over to Jake, who still stood by the open trunk. "What's the matter?"

"I'm not sure," Jake said. "I think it might be the battery."

The man's eyes darted from Cordelia to the car, then back to Jake. "Might be something else," he said. "Start it up."

Jake looked doubtful. "Guess it wouldn't hurt to try again." He went around the car to the driver's side. But as soon as he was inside, the man shoved Cordelia to the ground, grabbed Jake's backpack out of the trunk, and sprinted toward his truck.

"Stop!" Cordelia shrieked. She lunged to grab the thief's leg, but he slipped out of her grasp.

Jake jumped out of the car just as the man leaped into his truck. Luckily for the criminal, he had no trouble starting his beat-up clunker, and by the time Jake got to the road, all that was left of the Good Samaritan was a cloud of dust.

Jake let out a howl of obscenities while trying to gasp for air. "That dickhead!"

"Oh my God, Jake. I'm so sorry."

"He has my phone. And my wallet!" Jake crouched down and put his head in his hands for a minute before leaping up and blowing his top. "What the hell did you think you were doing, flagging down a total stranger like that? He could have killed us!"

"You were the one who said we could fix the car if someone came along with cables!" Cordelia shot back. How could Jake possibly blame this on her? She was only trying to help.

"Yeah, under normal circumstances! If there were plenty of cars going by and we weren't in the freaking desert!"

"Well, you didn't *say* that!"

"Does everything have to be spelled out for you? Molly always said you were the smart one!"

"Apparently not smart enough to avoid getting into your crappy car in the first place!" Cordelia yelled.

"Hey, I was doing you a favor!" Jake snarled.

"Go to hell!" she screamed.

"You know what, Cordelia? You suck!"

"No, *you* suck!"

She wanted nothing more than to storm out of there and never look back. Jake was being such an insufferable ass! But she had nowhere to storm to—she was stranded just as much as Jake was. Tears started to form in the corners of her eyes, the big fat drippy ones that she used to shed when devastating things happened. (Like when she was ten and Molly borrowed her Palm Pilot and left it on the bus and two days later, her dad took her to the beach and her precious glow-in-the-dark yellow Frisbee got carried away in the crashing waves. Hence, big fat drippy tears.)

She tried really, *really* hard to hold them back, but they just continued to stream down her cheeks. Stupid Jake! She should never have gotten into his car in the first place. No, it was her fault. She shouldn't have lost all her money. Why had she tried to impress Jake? Is that what she'd been doing? Why did she even care what he thought? And now she'd gotten his money stolen.

To make matters worse, she thought she'd been making some progress with Jake last night at the hotel. It seemed like they had almost been on the road to actually being friends. The night before, they didn't just force themselves to get along—they just kind of jelled, like they were comfortable and at ease. Maybe that's what Molly and Jake had felt toward each other. And maybe that's how she should feel toward Paul. But if that were the case, she wouldn't be so upset about Jacob Stein being mad at her or care that he was seeing her act like an emotional freak show. But she did care. She cared more than she knew she ought to. So she turned away from him and pulled her hair in front of her face. The thick strands of blond hair stuck to her skin and created some pretty decent camouflage. It was the only good thing to come out of the situation.

However, no matter how much Cordelia tried to hide it, she knew that *he* knew she was crying. She thought she had lost it all at the roulette wheel, but she'd never been more wrong in her life. Now, she really had nothing left, not even her pride.

*   *   *

Ten minutes and five gallons of tears later, Cordelia was officially burning up. The sun had gone from blazing to blistering, so she had proceeded to sweat through her pale blue striped Lacoste polo shirt. Her lips were in desperate need of some L'Occitane shea butter tinted lip balm, but that would mean going back into the car and facing a very bitter and ragged Jake. He'd locked himself in the Charger and begun pounding on the dashboard with his drumsticks after she'd cried for about 120 seconds. Which was fine by her. She didn't need his sympathy anyway. What she did need was water and lots of it. She'd packed a few liters in the car once she knew they were going to be driving through Death Valley—according to the brochure she picked up at the hotel on their way out, a lot of people become light-headed and dehydrated because of the heat, so it was recommended that travelers bring lots of water reserves in case of emergencies.

Cordelia was no idiot. This was a crisis. A flare-gun, hazard-lights, smoke-signal crisis. The water was in the backseat behind Jake. She needed liquid sustenance or else she would die. It was pretty clear that she'd have to interact with him again, even though it would hurt every fiber of her being.

Screw him, she thought. *If he wants to be a jackass, then fine.*

She strode up to the car and halted when she reached the driver's side. She saw the bottles of water on the floor behind Jake's seat. She was about to knock on his window and ask him to get up off his rump and do something useful like get her some water when the door opened and Jake came out...

...without his shirt on. Or his pants. Just a pair of plaid boxer shorts, stuck to his muscular thighs.

Cordelia jumped back and yelped. "What are you doing?"

Jake rolled his eyes. "Grow up, Cordy. We're in the center of an inferno and I'd prefer not to sweat to death."

She tried to avert her eyes, but it was like trying not to look at *Us Weekly* or *In Touch* when she stood in line with her mom at the grocery store—it was virtually impossible to resist. Jake could be the poster child for the Build Your Perfect Hot Guy Company, if such a thing should ever exist. She couldn't help but notice before, very casually, that he had been working out—his clothes fit more snugly than they used to and he seemed to walk with more purpose. When he'd dated Molly, he'd kind of slunk around as if he'd wanted to go unnoticed. But Cordelia had to admit, she detected a bunch of stuff about Jake's body, like the fact that it was a carbon copy of Matthew McConaughey's. His pectoral muscles had her completely hypnotized.

"Are you feeling any better?" he asked.

Cordelia looked over his shoulders so she could actually concentrate on what she would say, instead of salivating over how broad they were. "Like you give a crap."

Jake sighed and put his hands on his waist, drawing attention to his hip area, which was also mind-numbingly sexy. "Listen, I shouldn't have screamed at you like that. I was just angry."

"Whatever." She shrugged.

"I mean it, Cordy. That wasn't cool."

She could tell by the strained expression on his face that he did mean it, and that by the sturdiness of his legs, he had taken up long distance running, much to the delight of girls everywhere. "It's okay, you were just...a jerk."

"I know," he said remorsefully. "But you did something really risky and it backfired...*again.*"

Cordelia was about to defend herself, but she bit her lip. "I *suppose* I should have thought things through a little better."

"It was gutsy, though," he said, smiling. "Dumb, but gutsy."

She could feel herself softening a bit, like she was letting her guard down. "Well, I packed the car full of water when we left the hotel. How's that for being prepared and practical and focused on worst-case scenarios?"

Jake put both hands behind his head and laughed. Even his armpits looked amazing. "It's true. Without you, we'd be in much worse shape."

He leaned back over the seat and reached for a bottle of water. Cordelia got a real eyeful when he did, and she could feel her body temperature spiking.

"Here you go," he said, handing her a bottle.

The lukewarm wetness from the plastic felt good in her hands. "Thanks."

She chugged the water so quickly that she almost choked. Then she put the bottle up against her forehead, which cooled her down a little. "So what are we going to do now?"

"I don't know. This place is off the main road, so I doubt we'll be rescued anytime soon."

Cordelia frowned. "It's just so hot out."

"The sun will be going down in a few hours. We just have to make it until then."

"God, Paul is going to be worried," she muttered.

Jake looked puzzled. "Who?"

"My boyfriend, remember? We're headed to Yosemite to meet him."

"Right, right. The heat is doing things to me."

She glanced at his chest again. *It's doing things to me, too.*

Jake took Cordelia's bottle of water out of her hands unexpectedly and took a big gulp. "So how long have you lovebirds been together?"

"We're not lovebirds," she blurted.

Holy shit, did I just say that out loud?

"Okay, what are you?" Jake asked, handing her the water bottle again.

Cordelia just took it and stared at the squirt top. If she placed her mouth on it, it would be like putting her lips on Jake's....

Snap! Snap! Snap!

"Do you have *any* idea how annoying you are?" she said sourly.

"Well, then stop spacing out and answer my question."

"We're…you know…close."

"Wow, Cordy. That's sooooo lame." He snickered.

"Well, what about you and Molly? Were you two red-hot lov-ahs?" she replied.

"Are you kidding me? She was the most beautiful girl in the senior class," he said. "Homecoming queen, prom queen. I didn't stand a chance in hell with her."

Cordelia was confused. "Wait, you mean you guys never…uh–"

"Did the pokey-pokey?"

"Ew, Jake! She's my sister!"

Jake laughed so hard, he had to lean on Cordelia in order to hold himself up. The way the side of his body pushed against hers made everything from her pinkie toes to the tips of her ears tingle. He finally calmed down and wiped his eyes. "That really wigged you out, huh?"

"Let's just talk about something else," she said.

"Why? What are you afraid of?"

Cordelia was not about to back away from a challenge, especially when it came from Jacob Stein. "I'm not afraid of anything."

"Except flying," he corrected.

She narrowed her eyes. "I'm going to *kill* my mother." *If I survive this, that is.*

"She didn't tell me, Molly did," Jake confessed.

"What?"

"On our first date," he continued. "I couldn't believe

she said yes. I totally thought it was some sort of prank. Anyway, I took her to this cheap pizza place and then we walked on the beach. She kept telling me how much you loved it there, and that she was worried about you."

Cordelia was dumbfounded. "Worried about me? Why?"

"She told me that you'd won this smarty-pants award or something, and that you were asked to attend a fancy banquet in New York."

Her stomach grumbled at the memory of it. She'd been selected as a National Merit Scholar, along with Alexis Dunbar and five other students. She'd taken her PSATs a year early and scored in the top one percentile. Everyone had been so proud of her, and she'd really wanted to attend that ceremony in New York. But there'd been just one thing....

"You backed out because you wouldn't get on the plane," Jake said, shaking his head. "Molly said she was concerned that you'd miss out in life because you were too afraid to really face it."

Cordelia was very shaken by this admission. Not only had Molly never told her any of this, but she was amazed that her sister had even thought about things so deeply. Molly always seemed to be this flighty good-time girl, whose only concern was what pair of designer jeans she was going to wear to school or what boy was going to come after her next. She knew Molly was as sweet as they come, but she'd never exactly thought of her as contemplative or wise.

"After that, she took off all her clothes and ran into the ocean, screaming 'Cowabunga!'"

Cordelia doubled over in laughter. "You just gotta love Molly. What did you do?"

Jake smirked. "I got down on my knees and thanked God."

"I bet you did."

"But I didn't go skinny-dipping. I was too afraid."

She playfully elbowed Jake in the arm. "And you missed out."

"You're telling me," he said, grinning. "I was thinking about what you said to me, though. About being a hypocrite."

"Hold on a second. I want to enjoy this." She giggled.

"Ha-ha. Anyway, I thought I should tell you that I believe taking risks and letting go are good things, when you've made a conscious choice to do so and weighed all the options. Know what I mean?"

Cordelia's cheeks actually hurt from the wide smile that came across her face. "Yes, I think so. You're saying that balance is important in life."

"As important as breathing," Jake said, grabbing the water out of Cordelia's hand once again. This time his thumb grazed her palm, and that fluttering sensation from a few days ago came roaring back with a vengeance.

She tried that breathing thing of Paul's again, but strangely enough, it didn't work. So Cordelia closed her eyes, pretended that she was strolling along the sleepy California shore, and hoped that she would make it until sunset without hyperventilating. After all, Jake would be the only one around to resuscitate her....

Chapter Ten

Cordelia and Jake made it through the night and lived to see the next morning. It'd been her idea to stay in the car until dusk so that they'd be protected from the sun. But the heat had become so unbearable that Cordelia had changed into her red two-piece Tommy Hilfiger swimsuit. Jake had seemed very uneasy at the sight of Cordelia's overly exposed skin, so he'd quickly pulled out a deck of cards from his glove compartment and spent two hours teaching her how to play a mean game of blackjack. At sunset, they'd sat on the roof and munched on the remnants of a half-eaten package of mostly melted Twix, which Jake had found rolled up in a beach blanket in the trunk.

They'd talked about lots of insignificant stuff—

favorite movies (Jake's was *Kentucky Fried Movie* and Cordelia's was *Eternal Sunshine of the Spotless Mind*), the least edible food in the vegetable kingdom (Cordelia hated sprouts while Jake detested cauliflower), and best-looking celebrities (Jake lusted after Jessica Alba and Cordelia nearly fainted when she said Josh Duhamel's name). When it got dark, Cordelia crashed in the backseat while Jake snoozed in the front. Before they went to bed, Cordelia prayed that she'd wake up to some sort of miracle.

But all she'd gotten were lousy kinks in her neck and everywhere else in her body. She was so stiff from being cramped in a ball for seven hours that she could barely get out of the car. She felt pretty grubby, too. All that sweat from yesterday and she was nowhere near a shower. This was definitely not the work of angels.

Cordelia stood up and stretched, but was startled a bit when she spotted Jake working under the open hood of the car.

"What are you doing?" she asked.

He offered a rueful grin. "I don't know. I keep thinking that if I just look at the engine long enough, something will happen."

Cordelia ambled up beside him and peered under the hood. She pointed to a dangling loose wire. "What's that?"

"I don't know. Maybe it's a cable line."

"It looks like it should be connected to something," she remarked.

"How about the battery?" he asked. "Right over there."

She reached in and grabbed the wire.

"Watch out, your hands are going to get dirty," Jake said. "And you might be out of Purell."

Cordelia smirked. "I never run out." She moved her hands around the battery and felt something like a hole. Keeping one hand on that, she pulled the loose wire toward it. There was a click as it caught onto something, and then the wire became taut. She and Jake looked at each other.

Without a word, Jake hopped into the driver's seat. A second later, the engine was noisily throbbing. Cordelia slammed down the hood and got in the car.

"I have absolutely no idea what I just did!" she exclaimed.

"Neither do I," Jake replied. "But who cares? We're moving!"

"Cowabunga!" she shouted, and pumped her fist in the air.

"Now take your clothes off," he said jokingly.

Cordelia recoiled the instant he made that comment. She wrapped her arms around herself and shifted awkwardly in her seat.

"Jesus, Cordy. I was kidding." Jake shook his head and chuckled. "Your clothes can stay on if you want."

"I know, I'm just chilly from the sudden blast of AC," she lied.

He grimaced. "Right."

Cordelia dug into her bag and got out her snoozing Treo. She shook it a little bit, hoping that there was a tiny speck of juice left in it. Nope, nothing. There wasn't an outlet in sight either. She needed to call Paul, and fast, before he sent out a search party of park rangers to look for her.

"Did you sleep okay?" Jake asked. He was flooring the Charger now, but it still only went about sixty miles per hour.

"I guess," Cordelia said, grabbing the back of her neck, which was still extremely tight. "My neck kind of hurts."

"Yeah, I know what you mean. I've crashed back there many times and woken up feeling like total shit."

Then Jake took his right hand off the wheel of the car and put it on Cordelia's left shoulder. He began rubbing slowly at first, then worked his way to the back of her neck. She was shivering, and she knew it had absolutely nothing to do with the air-conditioning. His hand massaged her more intensely now, each circle he made with the palm of his hand felt so good. She closed her eyes and concentrated on how every cell in her body was releasing all of this built-up tension. Her lips began to moisten as Jake pressed harder on her skin. Her cheeks felt flushed, and she was clenching the muscles in her thighs.

"All better," Cordelia stammered, grabbing his hand.

"You sure? My hands can go on forever," he said.

She swallowed hard. "Really, I'm okay. Thanks."

"Suit yourself." Jake placed his hand back on the steering wheel. "Your sister always loved my back rubs."

Cordelia felt this burning sensation rise up in her chest. She couldn't believe this. Was she actually jealous of her sister...and Jacob Stein? She imagined herself pushing an eject button beneath her seat and soaring back home to San Diego.

"Well, I'm sure it wasn't agony for you," she snapped back. "Molly's so beautiful."

Jake said nothing for a minute, his eyes glued to the road. "She was always supremely sexy," he said finally. "And something else; I don't know how to describe it. Being with her was like...being at a party."

Cordelia nodded in affirmation. "Yes, Molly loves to party."

"No, that's not what I meant. Molly *is* a party. All by herself. And when I was with her, I felt like I'd been invited to Cirque du Soleil or something. She was always sparkling, you know? There was no darkness, no worry. All the bad stuff in the world, all the problems, they didn't touch her. It was like she was above and beyond all that. Nothing bothered her."

"So, if you were with Molly…nothing would bother you either."

Jake grinned. "Well, that's what you hoped for. Like maybe it was contagious. That she'd kind of rub off on you."

Another burning pang of jealousy stabbed at Cordelia's rib cage. "So, did she rub off on you? Did you forget all your problems?"

"No. I tried, though. I guess I'm still trying. It's probably why I act so—"

"Weird?" Cordelia said.

Jake sneered a little. "Um, I was going to say stress-free."

"Gotcha."

"You see, I did have problems. I still do," Jake continued.

"Everyone has problems," she said, but he didn't seem to hear her.

"And Molly didn't like that, especially if I talked about them. Even if I was just worrying about them silently, she could tell. She wanted me to be happy all the time. She'd tell me to cheer up, let it go, loosen up. Live in the moment."

"Like Paul." Cordelia didn't realize she'd spoken out loud till she heard Jake go, "Huh?"

"He's all about meditation, you know? He thinks we should all experience the here and now very deeply. He believes everyone should be one with the world."

"Interesting," Jake said.

"What?"

"I don't mean to sound like a dick, but from what you said, it seems that he expects everyone to do things his way. That's kind of self-indulgent and arrogant, don't you think?"

Cordelia sat there, unresponsive. She knew she should have jumped to Paul's defense, but she felt like there was some truth to Jake's observation, even though she wasn't entirely sure.

"Anyway, I tried to be what she wanted me to be. Only I couldn't. So she…" His voice trailed off.

"That's sad," she murmured.

"I'm over it," Jake said unconvincingly.

"I mean, I think it's sad when people can't be loved for who they are." She tried to put it in concrete terms. "Like, two people fall in love, okay? Then one of them tries to change the other one, to make him or her into someone else. Not the person that the person was to begin with. So why did they fall in love in the first place? Am I making any sense at all?"

Jake glanced at her. "I think I get what you're saying. What was the basis for the original attraction between two people? And why can't that be enough?"

"Yes! If you love someone, why would you want that person to change?"

Jake took his eyes off the road just long enough for

them to share a look of complete comprehension. Cordelia could feel a rush of exhilaration pass through her. It was as if they were really connected, like they totally *knew* each other. Then Cordelia quickly turned her head and glanced out her window, cutting the moment short.

Signs for Yosemite were popping up now, but Cordelia's eyes focused on one for a restaurant with a pay phone. She knew she had to call Paul and tell him they were almost there, even though the excitement she had felt about this visit had gone missing all of a sudden. And then she got a funny feeling, an odd sense of awareness, like she knew the exact place she'd lost it....

"Jake? Do me a favor. Pull over at that restaurant up ahead?"

"Sure, but I'm not shutting the car off."

She laughed. "I don't blame you."

"You must be starving," Jake said. "Sorry I didn't mention food earlier; I just thought you'd want to get to Paul as soon as possible, considering how *close* you guys are."

"Knock it off," she replied. "I have to call him collect so that he doesn't think I'm dead in a ditch."

"C'mon, you're with me."

"Exactly," Cordelia quipped. "Knowing him, he probably already has your picture up on *America's Most Wanted*."

"Sounds like a great guy. Can't wait to meet him," he said sarcastically.

Cordelia's eye twitched uncontrollably when she realized that she'd be spending the next day with Paul *and* Jake. Paul—the perfect guy. Paul, who she'd barely thought about in the last two days.

Chapter Eleven

n hour or two later, the Charger pulled up in front of the Yosemite National Park information booth. Paul raced to the car, practically tore the passenger door off its hinges, yanked Cordelia out of her seat, and threw his arms around her. He seemed thrilled and relieved to have her back in his arms; he had never squeezed her tighter.

Cordelia felt great, too. Paul was being as sweet as ever and he had this stubble on his cheeks that scratched her skin a little. It also made him look much older and wiser. He greeted her with his traditional "nose bump"— he'd take the tip of his nose and pat it against hers. She loved it when he did this.

However, there was one problem with their joyful

reunion. It was being monitored by a bunch of total strangers and, of course, Jacob Stein. While Paul planted kisses all over her face, his Eco Warrior Yosemite friends were circled around them as if they were observing a rare specimen of larvae or something. It made Cordelia really uncomfortable, so she bashfully buried her head in his chest.

She was usually okay with him being affectionate, but everything seemed so off-kilter at the moment. Cordelia could barely make sense of what was happening around her. Maybe it was lack of food, maybe it was lack of sleep, or maybe it was a lack of something more intangible. She wished Alexis were around. Then they could sit down and analyze everything that was going on much like they did during model UN.

Jake stayed in the car until the public display of affection was over. But then he resurfaced and she had the unnerving task of standing between her boyfriend and her worst-enemy-slash-sister's-ex-turned-semifriendly-acquaintance-who-also-happened-to-be-super-hot.

Paul reached out and shook Jake's hand. "Thanks for bringing her by, Jake. I wish you hadn't run into so much trouble."

"Not a problem," Jake said. "We just had some bad luck, that's all. But we're fine. Right, Cordy?"

She tried not to think about how her stomach was

tying itself into a fisherman's knot. "I'm just glad we're finally here."

Paul flashed a megawatt smile and took her hand in his. "Me too."

Cordelia began to relax more when she felt his fingers intertwined with hers. It was so nice how small and comforted and delicate she felt in Paul's presence. She hadn't really noticed that she missed it until just then. "So aren't you going to introduce us to your friends?"

"Of course," he replied. "This is my roommate, Stewart Blakeslee."

"Nice to meet you," said a rail-thin, shaggy-haired guy with glasses.

"And this is Maya-Angelou Reynolds," Paul said, gesturing to a beautiful dark-skinned girl with flowing braids in her hair.

"Hi there," she said. "I just go by Maya."

Cordelia flinched a bit when she heard Maya's voice, which was cold and harsh, unlike her soft, earthy exterior.

"Well, it's all set up. There's a vacant cabin in our employee housing area. Jake can stay there, and Cordy, you can bunk with Maya."

Maya rolled her eyes. "If you want. There are other cabins available too."

Paul kissed Cordelia on the top of her head. "Yeah, but I want to make sure she's safe, you know?"

Cordelia was shocked by Maya's expression. *Is she gagging?*

"Thanks for hooking us up, Paul," Jake said warmly. "So, how's life as an unappreciated groundskeeper and tour slave?"

Paul looked at Jake as if he'd done something distasteful like unzipped his pants and peed on a giant sequoia in Mariposa Grove. "Well, the work is hard, but it doesn't go unappreciated, that's for sure. We all play critical roles in the day-to-day functions of the park, which is one of the most visited in the country."

Jake shrugged. "Sweet."

"But I also get a lot of free time to do my own thing. Maya and I have already gone on some amazing hikes and done some birding...."

Cordelia didn't like the sound of that one bit, but she tried to stay positive. "Have you seen a red-legged honeycreeper?"

Stewart snickered. "A red-legged honeycreeper? Here?"

"No, you won't see one of those around Yosemite," Paul told her. "I did see a black-headed grosbeak yesterday."

"Fantastic!" Cordelia exclaimed.

"They're common to these parts," Maya said blandly.

"Okay, but...they're still nice birds to see, right?" She could tell she'd just said something dumb from the way Maya raised her eyebrows, which were in serious need of tweezing.

But at least Paul was gazing at her kindly. Cordelia smiled back at him. "I can see you're going to be happy here."

"It's an amazing place," Paul said, "filled with incredible beauty. The cliffs, the falls. I can't wait to show all of it to you."

Cordelia peered over her shoulder to check on how Jake was doing. He was kicking some pebbles on the ground with his feet and staring off into space. She knew he must have been feeling out of place there. In fact, she was feeling the exact same way. Even though Paul was trying to be welcoming, his friends seemed anything but impressed with her and they'd only just met.

"You guys must be hungry. Would you like some lunch?" Paul asked.

Jake's ears perked up and he joined in the conversation. "Man, I could go for a greasy, cardiac arrest–inducing burger."

"Oh my God, that sounds delicious." Cordelia rubbed her tummy in anticipation and giggled. But when she saw the disappointed look on Paul's face, she immediately frowned.

"Well, wouldn't you rather have a healthy salad with fresh organic vegetables?" he asked. "That's what all of us eat, and it's a really good source of fiber."

Jake stifled a laugh. "My fiber intake is great, thanks."

"But what about your cholesterol?" Stewart asked.

Maya shot Jake a dirty look. "And the fact that you're eating something that used to live and breathe and have a mother?"

Cordelia tried to derail this conversation before Jake could respond. "I'd love a yogurt or something."

Paul shook his head disapprovingly. "Yogurt is on our Do Not Eat list."

"Because it's made from milk," Maya clarified.

"What's wrong with milk?" Jake asked. "It's supposed to do a body good and all that crap."

Maya eyed him sternly. "It's not good for the cow. Have you ever seen an electric milking machine? It's torture for the animal. Even by hand, milking isn't right. Did you know that a cow has to be kept permanently pregnant to produce milk? How do you think a cow feels about that?"

Jake grimaced. "Gee, I don't know. I've never really had a conversation with a cow that went beyond *moo*."

Cordelia pressed her lips together to keep from laughing. It was obvious that no one else thought Jake's crack was funny, and now that she thought about it, she realized that a few days ago, she wouldn't have found it funny either. Since when did she get Jake's jokes? Since when did she feel this giddy when she looked at him from afar?

Maya's voice rose. "Just because a cow can't talk shouldn't mean she doesn't deserve a full and happy life! Did you know that a cow can live twenty, twenty-five years? A milk cow only lives five or six years. And do you know what happens to her after that? She's slaughtered and turned into your greasy burger!"

Stewart came to Maya's side and proclaimed, "There's also evidence that suggests that milk can cause cancer."

Jake nodded. "Well, of course, what doesn't?"

Cordelia couldn't figure out how he managed to keep a straight face. "Look, I can understand being a vegetarian. But if you can't have anything made out of milk, you can't have cheese either. So how do you get any protein? Just from eggs?"

Maya gasped in horror, but Paul calmly explained, "Vegans don't eat eggs, Cordy."

She was confused. "I've seen you eat eggs, Paul. I made omelets last week, remember?"

Stewart visibly shuddered.

Paul gave him an apologetic look before responding to Cordelia. "I've come to realize that being a vegetarian is a total cop-out. I'm vegan now. We avoid all kinds of cruelty to animals."

Cordelia could see that Jake's stoic face was about to crack. He scratched his head as if he was pondering something. "Eggs are animals?"

"Eggs are produced by animals," Maya replied. "We're against all kinds of animal exploitation."

Jake couldn't suppress his laughter anymore. "Oh, I get it now." He chuckled. "You won't eat an egg until a chicken gives you her permission."

Maya blinked rapidly and appeared ready to attack, but Paul was there to restrain her. "Jake, where you come from, it might be cool to make fun of people's beliefs," he said. "But that's not what we do here."

Suddenly, Cordelia found it necessary to step in and set things straight. "He's not making fun of anything, Paul. He's just making a joke."

Maya and Stewart exchanged annoyed glances while the grin on Jake's face widened immensely.

As for Paul, he seemed troubled. "There's a difference?"

"Well, you need a sense of humor to understand which is which," she said mockingly.

Everyone stood motionless, especially Cordelia, who was amazed that she'd said that in front of everyone. But she couldn't help herself. Jake was being cornered by these judgmental environmentalists, and Paul was just going along with it, which was so unfair. It reminded her of that time he'd criticized sunbathers and of other occasions when he'd made it very clear that other people were substandard because they didn't think like he did. It was an unappealing trait that she had blocked out of her mind most of the time, but now that it was directed at Jake, she wasn't able to ignore it for some reason.

But her perturbed attitude just seemed to go right

over Paul's head. "You're probably testy because you haven't had anything to eat. C'mon, this way."

He put his arm around her waist and motioned for everyone to follow him toward the cafeteria. But Cordelia noticed something very strange—he was kind of pushing her instead of guiding her along. It was so subtle, but she picked up on the pressure he was putting on her and it was making her feel weighed down and heavy. She could hear the footsteps behind her and wondered if Maya and Stewart were going to grab Jake and bury him alive somewhere so he could *really* commune with nature. She turned and looked back and caught Jake staring at her, wearing that trademark smirk of his.

Then she saw Jake mouth some words, and a lightness came over her entire body and made her feel as if she were soaring alongside a red-legged honeycreeper, or whatever birds were flying around the tops of the majestic trees at Yosemite these days.

"You are awesome."

*   *   *

Cordelia was psyched when Paul told her that he had taken the rest of the day off so they could wander around the park. It was just the diversion she needed. They drove around in a cool ATV so they could explore some of the more rugged, hard-to-reach areas. Paul knew the place as if he'd been born there. He was rattling off facts every time they passed something new. Cordelia adored his passionate spirit and how he lit up in this environment. When she took in all that she was seeing, she could understand why.

As they whizzed down Tioga Road—the trail that connected the Crane Flat and Tuolumne Meadows—she inhaled the fresh scent of all the blooming flowers. She loved the way the ripples in the lakes moved and committed to memory the image of the granite domes sparkling in the sun. She strolled through Yosemite Valley and snapped pictures of the gorgeous waterfalls, cliffs, and unusual rock formations with her digital camera. She hiked through the formidable Merced Groves, where she sought refuge in the shade of humongous sequoia trees.

But no matter what jaw-dropping, mind-blowing piece of scenery she encountered, Cordelia couldn't fully enjoy it because she was miserably preoccupied with thoughts of Jake. She felt horrible about leaving him behind in the hands of Maya and Stewart, the fascist über-granolas, yet he'd insisted that she and Paul have some "close time." Now she kept wondering what he was doing and if he was feeling overcome with confusing emotions, just as she was. Every waterfall that poured into a lagoon, every patch of chest-high wildflowers, every trail that wound its way through a canopy of grandiose trees—Cordelia searched herself and knew something didn't feel right. She just couldn't figure out what it was.

She looked up ahead to Paul, who was stepping on slippery rocks and steadying himself with a sturdy walking stick. He had such a commanding, confident presence that had the power to render her completely in awe. Yet it only took a few hours for Cordelia to piece a lot of things together—she didn't really feel protected when she was with Paul as she'd originally thought. Actually, she felt kind of inferior to him most of the time.

Also, Jake and she might have fought a lot, and he may have criticized her every move, but he'd always been very honest and straightforward about it, like he'd wanted her to come out of her shell, embrace the unexpected, and find her own way in the world. As for Paul, it seemed more and more like he was trying to get Cordelia to follow his path, not hers.

He paused for a second to catch his breath and sat down on what appeared to be a gigantic lava stone. "Phew, I'm beat. Want to take a break?"

"Not really. Actually, if we push on a little farther, we could get back to the park in a half hour," she said. She was secretly hoping that she could catch up to Jake.

"Cordy, we've been going nonstop for hours. You're going to be sore if we don't sit down."

"But I feel fine."

"I do this stuff all the time. I know what I'm talking about. You need to stretch your muscles and relieve any stress that's on your core."

Core? What am I, an apple?

"Okay, I'll sit for a minute," she said, giving in.

"Great," Paul said with a smile. He put one of his strong arms around her when she sat down next to him, then pulled her in for a deep, lingering kiss.

It was the same kind of soft, tongue-filled smooch that Cordelia remembered sharing with Paul the last time she saw him—on the steps of her house back in San Diego. A part of her wished she could go back in time and stay on the steps with Paul forever. But as Paul kissed her, she knew that they couldn't be that way again. She suddenly knew who she wished she could kiss—someone she never would. Jake. Despite herself, Cordelia felt tears welling in her eyes.

It was excruciating.

Paul moved his way down her neck. More tears gathered when she remembered how she used to absolutely love this. However, her boyfriend was too busy nuzzling her to notice how upset she was.

"I wish I could have you stay in my room tonight," he whispered. "But the others look up to me, you know?"

"It's okay," she said softly, trying to compose herself.

"Maybe later, I could come by Maya's room and we could sneak off somewhere secluded," he suggested.

Cordelia shuddered. Then Paul paused when he noticed that his T-shirt was getting damp from her tears.

She pulled away and wiped at her eyes. "I'm sorry, Paul."

"What's the matter, Cordy?"

"I don't know," she said. She couldn't be more succinct than that.

"God, I'm such a jerk." Paul went into his cargo shorts and pulled out a tissue for Cordelia. Even now, when she wasn't sure if she really wanted to be his girlfriend anymore, Paul was the most thoughtful guy she'd ever met. "You've had such a rough journey and I'm only thinking about...."

She blew her nose hard. "No, it's not you, Paul."

"Oh, I know that. It's *Jake*," he said tersely. "He's terrible!"

"What?"

"The guy's a clown," he went on. "I can't even imagine what it must be like for you, trapped in a car with that...I don't know what to call him. A fool without a clue? That seems about right."

Cordelia was totally taken aback by Paul's appearance at this very moment. He was actually ugly—his brow was crinkled, his sweet smile was submerged beneath an almost nasty sneer, the bright color drained from his eyes. This wasn't the look of jealousy either. It was the look of utter disdain, and for someone he barely knew. At least when Cordelia didn't like Jake, she had spent countless hours interacting with him—her hatred was based on some experience!

"Paul, don't you think you're making a snap judgment here? I mean, I know I complained a lot about Jake, but he's really—"

"Cordy, I'm an intuitive guy. Meditation can help me sense things about people that you can't possibly understand."

Wow. Wow. Woooooow.

"So you're saying that you've spent an hour with Jake and you understand him better than I do?"

"I'm highly observant. That's what happens when you really train your mind. Even so, it doesn't take a genius to see how screwed up he is. Not only are his ethics all out of whack, but he's also been putting you in danger. And he's a bad influence. I can't believe the size of that burger you ate during lunch. It was gross."

Cordelia couldn't believe what she was hearing. Sure, Jake had gotten her into some sticky situations, and true, some of it might have been because he lacked a sense of foresight. But it wasn't intentional, and at every turn, Jake seemed to be sincerely looking out for her. Paul was right about one thing, though. Jake was influencing her. He was showing her there was more to life than following her preconceived notions and tabulating things on her Treo. He was teaching her that the unplanned—the element of surprise—can be utterly exhilarating.

"That's not how it is at all," she said.

"Then how is it?" Paul asked, raising his eyebrow.

Cordelia's hands turned ice cold. He was giving her this wise look, like he knew something he wasn't supposed to know. Maybe Paul wasn't bullshitting. Maybe he was intuitive in a way she couldn't comprehend. She was scared that the instant she tried to explain, he'd be able to see right through her lavender ribbed tank top and into her soul.

Suddenly, a voice came from behind them.

"Hey, lovebirds."

Jacob Stein to the rescue, once again. Cordelia suddenly felt hot all over.

Paul stood up and grabbed his walking stick. "We were just heading back."

Cordelia shoved her snot-filled tissue into her khaki shorts. "Yeah, wanna come?"

Jake gave her a curious glance as Paul headed off down the trail without them. "Damn, did I just interrupt something?"

The sounds of Paul's footfalls got farther away and suddenly she was able to breathe a lot easier. "No, you didn't."

"Your eyes are all red, though," he said.

"Allergies," she replied quickly.

Jake smirked. "So that's why Nature Boy looks crushed."

Cordelia smiled at him, and they walked back toward the cabins together, matching each other stride for stride.

Chapter Twelve

The rest of the evening had been like the WordReference.com definition of "surreal." Everything had felt like a strange yet lucid dream. She'd had to endure four hours of campfire singing, which ended with a raucous version of her all-time favorite (*not!*) Woody Guthrie tune, "This Land Is Your Land." The only thing that had made it worthwhile had been watching Jake snag Maya's bongos so he could accompany Stewart's very mediocre acoustic guitar playing. Dinner had been even worse. Paul had made a cauliflower casserole. Its pungent aroma had made her and Jake nauseous, so they'd just had some whole-grain bread slathered with creamy organic peanut butter.

Then they'd all retired to their appropriate lodgings—

Jake had sauntered off to his private cabin while Cordelia had had to room with Maya, who was anything but enthused to have her around. Maya had practically ignored her for most of the night, with the exception of asking her when she was leaving. When both of the hands on her Swatch had hit twelve, Cordelia went to sleep wishing she would have hugged Jake good night, thinking about how many messages Molly had probably left on her Treo, and hoping Paul wouldn't come knocking on Maya's door.

Thankfully, Paul hadn't disturbed her, so she'd gotten in a full night of erratic tossing and turning. The next morning, Cordelia had a whole new day ahead of her, but she couldn't stop worrying about what her boyfriend had up his sleeve next. They were standing in an open field, and he had made her cover her eyes and promise not to peek.

Molly and Eureka were looking better and better with each passing minute.

"Don't look until I tell you to," Paul announced.

Great, another order, she thought.

"I don't really like surprises, remember?"

Cordelia bit her lip after she'd said that. If this had been Jake, maybe she would have been revved up for this. But he'd taken off by himself earlier that morning to rent a bike and do his own tour of the park.

"You'll like this one, I promise."

Suddenly, there was an incredibly strong gust of wind that almost knocked Cordelia on her butt. A whirring sound became louder and louder as the air whipped through her Anthropologie ruffled miniskirt like a tornado.

"What's going on?" she screamed above the deafening noise.

"Okay, open your eyes!" Paul shouted back.

Cordelia was in a state of sheer panic when she saw a helicopter landing a few yards away from them.

"It's a new thing we're trying out. Tourists love the helicopter rides over the Grand Canyon, so why not over Yosemite? It hasn't officially started yet, but I know the pilot, and he agreed to take us up," he yelled.

She choked back the taste of bile that was creeping up the back of her throat. When she found her voice, she shrieked, *"Are you crazy? I'M AFRAID OF FLYING!"*

Paul screeched into her ear, *"I know. This is exactly what you need, Cordy. Thirty minutes in a helicopter with me holding your hand. You'll get over your fear, and when you go back to San Diego from Eureka, you'll be able to take a plane!"*

The propeller kept whizzing above Cordelia's head. She could barely think straight. *"I can't do this, Paul. I'm serious. Call it off, okay?"*

But Paul continued to smile knowingly. *"Cordelia, listen to me. Fear is what traps people and keeps them from achieving their true potential."*

Her mind flashed back to the other day, when Jake had told her how Molly worried about her little sister. Maybe Paul was right. Maybe he knew her better than she knew herself.

"Going on this ride is the best way to deal with your fear of flying," he continued at full volume. *"You can't spend your life like this. Think of what you'll miss out on."*

It was eerie hearing Paul utter almost the exact same phrasing that Jake had used seventy-two hours ago.

"Hey, what's going on?"

Cordelia turned to see Jake leaping off his bike and running toward them.

"Don't worry about it, Jake! I have everything under control!" Paul shouted.

Jake glanced at Cordelia, who was visibly shaking. Her hands trembled and her teeth chattered. She looked as if someone had thrown her in a blender. *"She has a really bad fear of flying, man. You're not thinking of taking her up in this thing?"*

"It'll be fine," Paul yelled, and reached out for her hand. *"Let's go, Cordy."*

Cordelia's eyes began to fog over, so much so that she couldn't tell Jake from Paul. She just wobbled along behind whoever was yanking her arm and prayed that a bolt of lightning would strike the helicopter and the insanity would stop.

But something even better happened.

As Paul pushed Cordelia into the backseat of the cockpit, Jake hopped in next to her.

"I'm right here, Cordy. We're going to do this together, okay?" he said as he laced his fingers in between hers.

Cordelia's heart lodged in her throat. She couldn't say much of anything except for something that sounded like, "Gurgle."

Paul jammed himself in next to Jake without much of an argument. But when he saw that Jake was holding Cordelia's hand, he seemed very annoyed. *"Take her up, Bob."*

The pilot gave the crew a big thumbs-up, and suddenly Cordelia felt the helicopter rising off the ground. Her head began to spin as quickly as the propellers.

Maybe I can get through this alive. It's just mind over matter. Concentrate. No, don't concentrate. Let your thoughts drift away; pretend it's not happening. Wait, be zen. No, don't be zen. Don't be here now; be somewhere else in my head.

"Hey, are you (something incoherent)? *You just went* (something garbled)!*"

She wasn't even sure who was talking. Could be Paul or Jake, or maybe it was the pilot. Her hearing was getting as fuzzy as her vision. However, when she looked out the window, she was able to see that they were about a hundred feet off the ground. Immediately, her chest tightened as if she were having a heart attack.

"No, no, no…" Wait, was that *her* voice?

She thought she heard Paul. *"Cordelia, you can handle this! Stay centered."*

"Dude, she's freaking out." That was Jake, probably. *"We have to land this thing."*

She wanted to agree with whoever that was, but she couldn't speak. Her teeth were chattering so much that all she could do was moan.

"Cordelia, be strong," she heard Paul say, but she was sure she felt Jake's arms holding her tightly.

"That's enough," Jake said. *"Bob, could you bring us back down?"*

"No! She needs to do this; it's good for her," Paul snapped.

"Can't you see that she's terrified?" Jake said boldly. *"Take us down, now!"*

Cordelia didn't remember what happened after that, but the second the helicopter touched down and the pilot cut the engine, her mental faculties began to return to her. Jake picked her up and carried her out into the field. She held on to his neck very firmly, and he whispered into her ear: "I got you."

If she'd had any energy whatsoever, she would have kissed him.

Then all of a sudden Jake faked these wheezing noises, like he was out of breath. His knees buckled and they both came crumbling to the ground. Cordelia rolled a little bit in the grass, and Jake fell flat on his back.

"God, you're heavy. I'm surprised the helicopter

could even take off," he said while reaching over and poking her in the stomach.

It was kind of a mean joke, but when Cordelia saw the endearing look on Jake's face, she smiled. Then her smile turned into a giggle, which transformed into a series of laughs that were accompanied by the hiccups. Jake began laughing, too, and before long, he was in tears himself.

Paul appeared on the scene and peered down at them as they grabbed at their sides and gasped for air.

"Cordy, are you okay? You sound hysterical," he said with concern.

"It's just—Jake said something really funny," she blurted. She couldn't tell if she was laughing or crying, but she felt so...relieved.

Paul scratched his head in bewilderment. "I guess I'll tell Bob that we'll try again some other time."

For some reason, this set off the giggling once more. Jake snorted a few times, and this just made things worse. Paul shook his head and wandered back to the helicopter.

It dawned on Cordelia that her boyfriend had never made her laugh like this and that her sister's ex-boyfriend had somehow become a professional at it. She glanced at Jake, who was lying down on the grass with his hands behind his head. Then he looked back over at her and grinned.

"It's okay, Cordy. The clouds look fine from down here too," he said.

Her heart was still rattling inside her rib cage. She inched over a bit closer to him, so that her hip barely touched his. "I suppose they do. It's just…"

Jake took his hand and brushed a few stray hairs away from her face. "What? That Nature Boy wasn't able to get you over your fear?"

"I don't want to miss out on life," she burst out a little too loudly. She'd never had such mixed-up emotions. Cordelia couldn't even tell if she was panicking or if she was, well, more excited to be alive than she'd ever been before.

"Remember what I said about risks? They're better when they're calculated," he said, returning his gaze to the sky. "You'll know when you're ready."

Cordelia closed her eyes and felt the crisp breeze nipping at her earlobes. Her heart suddenly calmed down and her hands, which had been balled into fists, opened up and relaxed. Her mind was devoid of anxiety, and all she could feel was the warm California sun showering her with affection.

You'll know when you're ready.…

*   *   *

Cordelia took her noontime "recover from the near-death

experience" shower and scrubbed herself with Bliss Lemon and Sage Soapy Sap. Then she dried herself off, put on some fresh clothes (a pair of dark indigo Joe's Jeans and a cute J. Crew paper-thin T-shirt), and made a solemn vow to break up with Paul Morgan. At first, she thought that cleaning herself off would help build her confidence and convince her that she was doing the right thing. But as she wandered through the cabins and approached the spot where she and Paul were supposed to meet, that theory went out the window. She was nervous as hell and wringing her hands so strongly that reddish welts were appearing on her skin.

You can do this, she kept saying to herself. *You just need to say it real quick: "Paul, you and I just don't belong together."*

The more she tried to rationalize, the more she felt the urge to empty the contents of her stomach into the nearest recycling bin. She held herself still for a moment and thought about what was about to happen and why she was so terrified. Was it because she was afraid of how Paul might react? Was she scared that she might regret breaking up with him? Could be. The only other boy she'd ever dumped was David Decker, Alexis Dunbar's ex-boyfriend—Alexis was too afraid to do it herself, so she asked Cordelia to drop the bomb on him after their Science Olympiad competition. He never made another solar-powered scooter again.

Then the suspicion that her fears were actually Jake-related grabbed hold of her and wouldn't let go.

God, this is not *about Jake,* Cordelia reminded herself. *It's about Paul not being the right person for you.*

Anyway, Jake was, and always would be, her sister's ex-boyfriend. Not to mention obnoxious, rude, and *so* not her type. Case closed.

As Cordelia approached the campsite where the folk-singing jamboree had congregated the night before, she spotted Paul. She took a deep breath and began to walk toward him when she noticed that he wasn't alone. Maya was there. She ducked behind a tree and tried to get a better view, carefully trying not to disturb them. They were both on their hands and knees, crawling around trees and scouring through abandoned charcoal pits.

"I found one," Maya yelped.

Cordelia caught a glimpse of something shiny in her hand.

"What is it?" Paul asked.

"A chewing gum wrapper," Maya proclaimed.

"That's two points," he replied.

They're picking up litter together, she thought. *As a game?*

"Yay!" Maya looked so happy and animated, Cordelia could barely recognize her. "Hey, maybe we could incorporate this game in our tours. While people are admiring the sights, they could be looking for all those tiny things that the groundskeepers might have missed."

"That's brilliant!" Paul exclaimed. "We could make it a contest. Whoever gathers the most points could get something, like a free pass to the Wawona Hotel or something like that."

Now Maya sounded doubtful. "I don't know, Paul. Maybe we shouldn't turn it into a competition for prizes. Wouldn't that conflict with the notion that we have an obligation to the Earth? That we shouldn't expect to be paid to protect our planet?"

"That's a good point," Paul said. "But on the other hand, it may be years and years before people accept that. The Earth will suffer in the meantime. So I think the competition is justified."

Even from this distance, Cordelia thought she could see how Maya's eyes were shining. "Oh, Paul, you always seem to know the right way."

Cordelia was mesmerized. Maya truly worshipped Paul in a way that she could never duplicate. Here was a girl who appreciated him and shared all his values and even enjoyed crawling around in the dirt looking for garbage in order to be with him. And suddenly she understood Maya. All her crabbiness was actually jealousy.

She knew she should be feeling a stab of jealousy, too—that heartburnlike sensation that she'd felt when she heard Jake talk about giving Molly back rubs. She was thinking about it now and it still made her squirm. It was all there in black and white. Paul deserved a Maya, and Cordelia deserved…she couldn't bring herself to follow where that train of thought led.

Maybe she was just doomed when it came to boys. Maybe Molly had gotten all the boyfriend genes in the family. Cordelia felt miserable all over again, but she knew what she had to do.

She came out from behind the tree and started down the slope. Maya noticed her first, and Cordelia saw all the joy vanish from the girl's face.

"What are you guys doing?" she asked.

Paul got up and gave her a limp hug. She wasn't too sure that he was happy to see her. "We're just playing a game."

"Would you like to join us?" Maya asked snidely.

Now that Cordelia really knew where Maya's crabby attitude was coming from, she wasn't offended at all.

"No, thanks. Actually, Paul, could we take a walk?"

"Sure," he said, and took her hand. "There's a pretty waterfall that way."

"Great," she replied as they started off in an easterly direction, leaving Maya behind to play a solo version of the trash game. "Will she be okay?"

"Yes, I'm sure we won't be long," Paul said suspiciously. "That is, unless you think Jake might want to join us?"

Holy shit.

Cordelia was stunned. Paul was right—he was one

perceptive son of a bitch. Although he hadn't put it in those terms exactly. Whatever. He seemed to know what was on her mind, which meant there was no reason to drag this out any longer. If only Cordelia could get the words out. This was a time she *really* wanted her Treo handy. She could have prepared for this and had a bunch of backup breakup lines ready in case she choked.

Oh well, I guess I'm on my own.

Silently, they continued along a path, the huge sequoias rising above them. She tried to recall the conversation she'd had with Jake in the Charger about how Molly had wanted him to change. Jake had tried, but finally he'd realized he couldn't be someone he wasn't, and despite the fact that he adored Molly, he didn't want to be someone else if that's what it took to make her happy. Molly needed a person who wouldn't have to change. So did Paul, and so did Cordelia.

He stopped her when they reached the waterfall and looked directly into her eyes. "Okay, you can tell me what's wrong now."

She stammered for a second before getting right to the point. "Paul, I think you're a wonderful person," she said.

"So are you."

"But I've been doing a lot of thinking and I'm just not sure we're the perfect match for each other," she said while wiping her brow from heat and stress-induced perspiration.

"Is this about what happened earlier today?" Paul asked. "Sometimes my enthusiasm gets the best of me."

"Well, what I'm trying to say is—"

"I understand, Cordy," he interrupted.

She put her hands on her hips and stared him down. Now he wasn't even letting her break up with him the way she wanted to. "But you haven't let me finish, Paul."

"That's all right," he said sadly. "I've heard plenty."

"I just want you to have someone who clicks with you better, like Maya for instance," she added.

"Maya?" Paul immediately crossed his arms over his chest and began averting his eyes. "What do you mean, Maya?"

Cordelia smirked. "She really likes you. I can tell."

He cracked his knuckles nervously. "She's just interested in the ecological movement here, that's all."

"C'mon, Paul. If you're so intuitive, you had to have known this before I figured it out."

"Maybe," he said, grinning a little.

"Well, perhaps there's something to explore with her," Cordelia suggested, hoping to soften the blow.

"Kind of like you and Jake?" he countered.

Cordelia suddenly began to cough uncontrollably.

"No, of course not. We're just…" She paused and tried to come up with the right way to classify them, but Paul beat her to it.

"The perfect match?"

"I don't know, Paul," she said truthfully. "I wish I did, actually. This would be a lot easier."

Paul closed in on her and placed a tender kiss on her forehead, kind of like her father used to when she was little. "I'm not going to lie. I'm going to miss you."

Cordelia gazed up at him as if he were one of the gigantic trees he loved so much. "We don't have to miss each other. We could be friends."

"That sounds nice." He smiled and reached for his back pocket. "Know what friends do? Lend other friends some money so they're not traveling around broke."

"No, Paul. I couldn't take your money," she said bashfully.

"Because you just shot me down like a gangsta?" he replied.

Cordelia threw her head back and laughed. "Oh my God, you do have a sense of humor!"

Paul put a few twenty-dollar bills in the palm of her hand. "And you have just as much intuition as I do. Here's some good advice. You listening?"

She nodded her head.

"Don't ignore it."

Cordelia put her arms around him and gave him a big hug. "I won't. I promise."

Strangely enough, Paul didn't tell her how she should be feeling or what she should do next. That was going to be entirely up to her.

Chapter Thirteen

They'd been on the road for five hours, and Cordelia had limited her conversation with Jake to very simple one-word answers to his questions. She was worried that if she allowed herself to say anything more than that, she might blurt out something cheesy, like how she'd been studying the cute dimple in his chin for the past two hundred miles.

"You're awfully quiet today," Jake said. "Anything wrong?"

"No," she replied.

Good, I'm still safe.

They were approaching the coast now, and a whole new vista rose before them. The Pacific Ocean came into view and Cordelia's mouth dropped open in awe. It was like she hadn't been near the water in years. She noticed how the northern California coastline was a lot different from the one at home. There weren't many long stretches of white sand beaches dotted with sun worshippers. In fact, she saw hardly any people at all. There were plenty of waves, though, crashing against the rugged cliffs, sending showers of white foam cascading over the rocks.

"Do you want to pull over?" he asked.

Cordelia knew that doing so would just delay their arrival in Eureka and that she'd be sitting alone with Jake and her strangely lustful thoughts, which involved the two of them mixing it up in the shallow end of the surf. Maybe she truly *was* losing her mind. If they kept driving and got to Molly's, she'd at least have a buffer to keep her from doing anything stupid, like throwing herself at Jake's Converse-clad feet. But the sound of the roaring tide drowned out all of the little voices, which were telling her to be cautious and pragmatic. Stopping unexpectedly would be a "calculated risk"—one Jake was obviously willing to take. Maybe he was trying to tell her something. Maybe it was a sign.

Cordelia sharply drew in her breath. "Yes, I'd love to."

"Great," Jake said. "I've got a bunch of healthy food in the trunk. Stewart gave it to me. I think we formed some sort of special bond."

Lucky Stewart, she thought.

As Jake drove the Charger down a steep embankment, Cordelia had a brief flash of panic when she remembered what had happened in Death Valley. This car had a tendency to flatline every other time it stopped for a rest. The type-A girl she was last week would have nagged Jake about taking a safer road or pulled out her Treo and called up a list of the closest hospitals in case one of them got injured by an exotic jellyfish or something.

But now the only thought in her mind was how to stop imagining kissing Jacob Stein.

After they parked on an isolated section of beach, Cordelia and Jake sat on the hood of the Charger and began devouring healthy fare like trail mix (the kind without M&M's, unfortunately) and Quaker rice cakes. Cordelia tried not to obsess over the way his Adam's apple jiggled when he swallowed and she shoved countless handfuls of sunflower seeds into her mouth so she wouldn't have to talk. But her efforts meant nothing. She could barely take her eyes off him or avoid speaking.

"Slow down, Cordy. You're not eating tacos," Jake said, laughing.

She swallowed hard. "Shut up, jerk!"

He playfully nudged her with his elbow. "I bet your boyfriend would be thrilled that you're not sinking your teeth into any animal flesh."

Cordelia hesitated and bit her lip before giving him the latest news. "Actually, Paul isn't my boyfriend anymore."

Jake gave her a look that was a cross between a frown and a grin. "Shit, really?"

"Yeah, things weren't working out," she said, trying to gauge just how much Jake cared about her newly-single status.

But his expression was rather blank at the moment. "Want to talk about it?"

She chomped on some more sunflower seeds and gazed at the writhing ocean. "Well, we had a long talk, and I told him I wanted to be friends, but—"

"Wait a minute, I just remembered something I left in the trunk," Jake interjected, and bolted to the rear of the Charger.

Cordelia sighed. Any hope that Jake would be interested in taking her as his love slave had gone up in a fury of flames. She told herself that she should just forget all about it. She needed to keep her mind—and hands—off Jake or else face the ultimate consequence: betraying her loyalty to Molly.

He returned a minute later with an elegant pillow-case stuffed with God knows what.

"Okay, what did you steal from Mandalay Bay?" she asked.

He pulled a tiny bottle of alcohol from the pillowcase. "I took eight of these from the minibar. Jamaican rum."

"Why am I not surprised?"

"These aren't for me, if that's what you're thinking." He handed the bottle to Cordelia. "I figured you might want to drown your sorrows."

She eyed the bottle dubiously. Molly had referred to alcohol as "truth serum" enough times for her to know that if she drank one or two of those babies, she might confess all of her weird-as-hell feelings for Jake once and for all. But if she didn't loosen up soon, she might leap into the Pacific and float all the way to China, where she wouldn't have to stare at Jake's long, enticing fingers and the sexy curve between his square jaw and his neck....

She took the rum from Jake and gulped it down. It burned a little, but it also felt as warm as the Pacific in August.

"Any better?" he asked.

"Not yet."

"Give it a few minutes." Jake sat back down on the hood of the Charger, but this time his arm was now within an inch of Cordelia's. "Now what were you saying before? Something about being friends with Paul."

She sipped from the bottle a second time and finished off its contents. "Yeah, I'd like to stay friends, sure."

"Well, what made you decide that you didn't want to be with him?" he inquired. "Was it the helicopter thing?"

Cordelia was certain that she wasn't hallucinating.

Jake's upper arm had just touched hers! And it didn't just graze by—his flesh was still against her flesh!

"No, well…sort of. I don't know, there were a lot of things that weren't right," she replied, shifting her weight slightly so that her arm gently rubbed against his. The electric vibe that was coursing through her brain was now traveling to every sensory receptor north of her belly button. It was only a matter of milliseconds before it headed south of the border.

Jake snickered and pushed his knee against hers. "Like the fact that he was a douche bag?"

Cordelia caught that subtle movement too. He was totally, undoubtedly flirting with her…wasn't he?

"Stop, he was nice." She leaned over Jake, reached into the pillowcase, and pulled out another bottle. "He was just—"

"Pretentious? Self-righteous? Dull as a twenty-year-old kitchen knife?"

Cordelia playfully shoved him aside and when Jake bounced back from it, their arms were practically glued together. "Come on, Jake. That's not nice."

He peered down at his sneakers. "Yeah, well, you know me. I'm just a fool without a clue."

She choked on her rum so hard that Jake had to pat her on the back until she calmed down. "I'm so sorry that you heard that."

"Don't be. It's what most people think about me anyway," Jake replied coolly.

"Not me." The words were floating off her tongue now. Believe it or not, she was already a bit light-headed, which wasn't necessarily a bad thing.

"Please. You're practically president of the I Hate Jacob Stein Club!"

"Well, you were trying to take down the Cordelia Packer regime like you had a death wish or something," she quipped.

"Fair enough," Jake said, shoving another fistful of trail mix in his mouth. "But Paul's right about one thing: I don't have a clue."

Cordelia gulped back the rest of her rum. "Don't listen to him, Jake. He was picking up trash...*as a game!*"

He laughed really loudly. "And you didn't run off with him and elope? I'm shocked!"

She shoved him again and afterward he threw his arm around her and gave her a half hug.

"I'll stop making fun of you now," he said.

She could actually feel her eyes twinkling as they gazed into his. "Thanks."

There was a silence between them, yet it was anything but uncomfortable. She was just taking him in, as if she were making a map of all the distinctive qualities of his face—Jake's forehead had puckered to the point where his dark, thick eyebrows had almost come together, and he was smiling so widely that she could see his teeth were a wee bit crooked. Jake didn't flinch as she stared at him either. He returned her gaze and then some. Cordelia could feel the intensity of his look over-whelming her. She leaned in a bit and hoped he would meet her in the middle with a kiss that would send her flying into space without any fear.

But all he did was recoil.

"I think I need a drink too. Just one." He opened another little bottle of rum and chugged it. "You want some more?"

Cordelia's liquid courage was coming to a head. "Why the hell not?"

"Good answer." He snickered and handed her another bottle. "Cordy, can I tell you a secret?"

She held her breath and steadied herself on the Charger—things were beginning to spin a bit. "Sure, you can tell me anything."

Jake sighed. "My life is a fucking mess! I don't even know where I'm going to school in the fall."

The buzzing in her head was getting increasingly louder. "Aren't you checking out a school in Seattle?"

"Yeah, but checking it out for what? I studied all the time, but my grades were always average. I don't know what I want to major in. And why am I focusing on Seattle? Because I like the city?"

"There's still a killer music scene."

"Yeah, but I don't have any talent."

Cordelia grabbed his hand without any hesitation whatsoever. It was brave, it was bold, and he didn't let go.

"Jake, you're more than talented. You're like...um....Zach Hanson!"

He laughed so hard that he nearly fell off the Charger. "I was hoping you'd compare me to Keith Moon."

"Who?"

"Exactly," Jake said, giggling.

But the joke went over her head and through her head and around her head. In fact, she wasn't too sure that her head was even connected to her neck anymore. "Jake, I think I'm getting a buzz."

He shrugged. "So what? You're not driving."

Cordelia examined her drink thoughtfully. "I've never had a buzz before."

"You're kidding." Jake radiated disbelief. "Molly Packer's sister's never had a buzz?"

She took another gulp and wiped her mouth with the back of her hand. She knew it wasn't the classiest thing to do, but Jake had done much worse in her presence. Besides, it's not like she had much control over what she was doing right now, and that was more than fine with her.

"When we were in high school," Cordelia said, hiccupping, "and our parents were out, Molly's friends would come over with twelve-packs of beer. She'd ask me if I wanted to hang with them, but I wouldn't. God, I'm such a boring wuss!"

"You're not a wuss," Jake said flatly. "And you're

definitely not boring. In fact, you're a more interesting person than Molly."

She shook her head. "I sincerely doubt that."

"Molly and I never had conversations like this. We laughed a lot about goofy stuff, but I don't remember ever really talking about anything *real*."

"But she's so much more fun than me!" she shrieked, then flopped her head on Jake's shapely shoulder.

"Are you kidding? I don't think I've had more consecutive fun-filled days since I followed Pedro the Lion on tour."

She lifted her head up and gave him a peculiar look. "Don't toy with me, Jake."

He was still holding her hand, so he squeezed it a little. "I mean it. You're just as fun as Molly. Even more so, because there's no way that girl would have lasted ten minutes in Death Valley."

Cordelia's heart filled with so much joy, she thought she was about to combust.

Jake opened another bottle of rum and drank it swiftly. "Listen, this is just one guy's opinion, but maybe you're a little too concerned about how you measure up to Molly."

She set her drink down and stared at him.

"I've seen you when you let your guard down and set the rules and regulations for your life aside for a while," he continued. "You seem like you're—"

"More balanced?"

"I was going to say happier," Jake said. "And prettier even."

Impulsively, she embraced Jake and wrapped him in an airtight hug. She felt warm and excited, and he must have felt the same way, because he didn't pull away. In fact, he nuzzled his mouth into the nape of her neck and his hands gripped her waist.

This is it, she thought. *I'm ready.*

Cordelia didn't wait for Jake to meet her halfway (maybe the Jamaican rum made her impatient—it was difficult for her to tell). She ran her fingers through his thick, wavy hair and brought him in for a soft, yet brief kiss. But it almost felt like it hadn't happened because Jake was so tense. He barely moved at all. It was as if he'd been zapped with a stun gun.

She tried again and pressed her lips against his with a little more force this time. They were moist and delicious and tasted like a blend of raisins and cashews. Salty and sweet simultaneously!

Jake's body loosened and he began to kiss her back. Cordelia felt his tongue skim hers and his hands moved up to her cheeks. Her hands were occupied too—they were exploring every inch of him, caressing his back, rubbing his stomach, grabbing his thighs. Jake's mouth was getting hungrier and she felt his fingers pulling up the front of her T-shirt.

Without warning, Cordelia's pulse accelerated to a speed that could only be described as Mach sixteen. She could barely register how she was feeling. All she knew was that this was the happiest and the prettiest that she'd felt in her entire life.

And then it all came to a screeching halt.

Jake suddenly jumped up as if he'd been bitten and took a few steps away from her. "Cordy, we've gotta stop."

She gasped at the worried tone of his voice. "Why?"

"You're kind of drunk and tomorrow you might regret all of this," he said, turning his back to her so that he was facing the water.

Cordelia came up behind him and wrapped her arms around his torso. "I would have regretted it more if I hadn't done it."

Jake squirmed away and looked at her. The fresh smell of the sea air enveloped them, and the sounds of the water creeping up onto the shore echoed in Cordelia's ears. She was more terrified about what was going to come next than she'd been in that goddamn helicopter.

"I'm going to take a walk," he said gently. "I should find a phone and call your sister. Tell her we'll be in tomorrow morning, you know, once everything's gone back to normal."

The only thing Cordelia could do was nod her head. She watched Jake stroll along the seashells until he was out of sight. Then she fell to her knees and sobbed as if she had lost her favorite yellow glow-in-the-dark Frisbee in the ocean all over again. Except this time, she'd lost the guy who she knew belonged with her.

Chapter Fourteen

Cordelia had thought standing between Jake and Paul was awkward, but that had been nothing compared to watching Molly say, "Hello, how are you?" to Jake with some good old-fashioned groping. She could feel her body becoming feverish and her muscles turning rigid, which in some respects was a good thing. On the drive over that morning, she and Jake had barely said anything to each other. Jake seemed as if he'd lost his voice—he was clearing his throat incessantly—while Cordelia had felt completely numb from crying all night long and trying to pretend like she wasn't. She and Jake had had to sleep in the car again, and she didn't want him to hear her sniffling like a brokenhearted loser, so she'd proceeded to fake-sneeze for hours. He hadn't said "God bless you" even once—it was a terrible omen, indeed.

Now she was sitting on top of her sister's nearly refrigerator-sized suitcase and listening to Molly (who wore a lime green Malia Mills bikini top and a pair of white terry-cloth shorts that barely covered her butt cheeks) fawn all over Jake like he was a new Prada bag.

"Oh my God, you turned into a total hottie!" Molly screamed with pure delight.

Jake stepped back and looked at Molly with obvious approval. "You're looking mighty fine, too, girl. But you always do."

Jesus Christ, Cordelia thought. *Why don't they just do it right here on the steps?* It was so difficult for her to see them act all gooey with each other, especially because of how Jake had turned her down the night before. Cordelia had suspected that he might still have feelings for her big sister, but now it seemed undoubtedly true. She closed her eyes and wished for an earthquake to come along and shake them out of their gut-wrenching gushfest.

"I can't believe you waited until *after* we broke up to get all gorgeous on me," Molly said while flipping her hair flirtatiously.

"Serves you right for dumping my ass," Jake replied.

Cordelia rolled her eyes and forced her way between them. "Hey, Molly, remember me? The sister who's here to spend the summer with you?"

Molly giggled ferociously and hugged Cordelia. "Hiya, honey. I'm so happy you're here!"

Yeah, right, she thought. *More like can't wait to get rid of me so she can slobber over Jake.*

Her sister's face turned serious as she held Cordelia's hand. "You know, I was really worried about you. Thank God Jake called me last night. I left a ton of messages on your Treo. I was minutes away from, like, issuing an Amber Alert. What happened out there?"

Suddenly, Cordelia felt a flurry of emotions, the first of which was remorse. Here she was thinking the worst of Molly's intentions, when in reality she was concerned about what had happened to her kid sister. The second, third, fourth, and fifth emotions were all the same one: guilt. If Cordelia told Molly about "what happened out there," she might go into a rage and club Cordelia to death with her signature pair of red Kors espadrilles.

Jake glanced at Cordelia quickly and then shrugged his shoulders. "We had some car troubles, that's all."

Car troubles! Is that what guys call making out *these days?* Cordelia couldn't help but feel really insulted. Sure, that was kind of what happened, but didn't the previous night mean anything to him? She could have sworn by the way he'd kissed her that there was some magnetic attraction between them. Actually, it was more than just attraction—it was an undeniable connection, except for the fact that Jake seemed all too happy to deny that they'd ever gone lip-to-lip. She was too hurt to hold back her anger.

"Yeah, well, maybe if Jake had enough common sense to drive a reliable car, we wouldn't have had that problem."

Molly nudged her. "That was pretty mean."

"No, she's right. What do I know about being reliable?" Jake said coolly. "Cordy's the authority on that subject and everything else. And she *never* makes mistakes."

Cordelia pushed Molly aside and squared off against him, just like old times. "Well, being reliable is certainly better than letting people think that you're one way when you're actually something else altogether."

Jake looked at her, confused. "What the hell are you talking about?"

"Oh, you know what I mean," she said with a sneer.

"No, I don't," he barked. "That made no sense."

"It made *perfect* sense!" she shouted. "Molly, what did I just say?"

Molly's face became pinched as if she'd just swallowed a lemon. "Sorry, sis. You lost me at 'reliable.'"

Jake's stern expression suddenly broke into a smile. Then he chuckled a bit, which made Molly giggle like an elf. Soon, they were laughing so hard that tears were running down their cheeks. Cordelia tried to force a halfhearted grin, but on the inside, she was crumbling into a pile of confetti.

Molly wiped her eyes once she was done laughing. "You guys must be hungry. Want to hit a diner? There are tons of cheap places around here since Eureka's a college town."

"Sounds awesome," Jake said.

"Then you can tell me all your road stories." Molly clapped her hands together as if she were applauding.

Cordelia shuddered nervously. "Can I take a shower first?"

"You and your showers," Molly said, and put her arm around Cordelia. "Just don't take forever in there. Jake doesn't like to be kept waiting."

She growled and dragged her bags through the front door. "Yeah, whatever."

Molly and Jake followed her into the bachelorette pad, which was bedazzled with glittery pink fabrics. The walls were painted a bold shade of fuchsia. The shag rugs were in the shape of hearts, and a beaded curtain hung in the middle of the living room.

"Better than my VIP suite back home, huh, Cordy?" Molly said proudly.

Cordelia managed to smile at the Mollyness of it all. "Way better, sis. You do all this yourself?"

"Some of my male admirers helped me out," Molly replied.

Jake plopped down on a huge plush Love Sac chair. "How many are there now? Five? Ten?"

Molly leaped in next to him. "Don't worry, none of them could ever replace you."

Cordelia had to dig deep and will herself not to throw up. "I kind of lost my appetite. Maybe you should just go ahead to breakfast."

Jake tried to wiggle out of the chair, but Molly had him trapped. "Don't be ridiculous. Come with us," he said.

Cordelia searched his face and realized he was being sincere. He did want her to go with them, but for what? To watch him and Molly laugh and cry and be all BFF with each other? She just knew she wouldn't be able to handle it. Reliving how Jake had dissed her less than twelve hours ago over and over again in her mind was torture enough.

"Really, go ahead," she said wistfully. "I'm tired so it's probably better if I just wash up and crash in the room."

Molly popped up and grabbed her purse off the kitchen table. "Okay, sis. Just push back the beads and your AeroBed is ready to go."

Cordelia sighed. Forget about trying to study for that class of hers. Obviously, she'd be sleeping in the Molly Packer Party Central thoroughfare for weeks, not getting any shut-eye whatsoever.

"Want me to bring you back something?" Jake asked Cordelia as Molly bolted out the front door.

She couldn't bring herself to speak to him. She knew that she was one syllable away from wailing like a toddler, so she just shook her head.

"Jakey! I'm not getting any younger!" she heard Molly call out.

He turned on his heels and walked away. Surprisingly, Cordelia was relieved, because now she was alone and didn't have to pretend that she wasn't crying.

* * *

Cordelia spent the next two hours in organization utopia. She finally was someplace that she could recharge her Treo and access her e-mail, to-do lists, and Outlook calendar. So after taking that shower, she sprawled out over her AeroBed and attempted to plan out the rest of her summer. There would be no more surprises, no more unexpected turns-of-events, and definitely, absolutely no more "calculated risks." She was going to regroup and restructure and coordinate and overthink her way out of this enormous funk she was in. Once she established a routine, everything would fall into place. She'd be in control again and that would be *much* better than any kind of fun she might have had while experiencing how the other, less-structured half lived.

But as much as she wanted to focus on assembling her summer reading catalog, which she was downloading off the Humboldt State University Web site, Cordelia wasn't able to shake thoughts of Jake feeding Molly blueberry pancakes and dousing her with maple syrup á la her sister's favorite soft porn classic, *9 1/2 Weeks*. She also kept flashing back to that fantastic kiss she and Jake had shared on the beach. The way his thumbs had pressed up against the bare skin of her stomach. The way his lips moved urgently against hers. The way his body responded so well to her touch—it was all so perfect. Better than perfect, actually. It was…

Cordelia's reverie was interrupted by the slam of the front door.

"And then she kneed Mike right in the balls," she heard Jake say.

"Oh my God, she didn't!" Molly replied.

"Yeah, when I showed up he was rolling around on the floor in agony."

Molly let out a hyena laugh. "That's so hilarious. Cordy, get out here!"

She begrudgingly hoisted herself off the AeroBed and peeked out through the beaded curtain.

"Jake was just telling me about all of your exploits," Molly said, grabbing Cordelia by the arm.

All but one of them, I bet, she thought.

"I can't believe you lost all your money gambling. That's so unlike you, Little Miss Responsible," Molly added.

Jake looked at Cordelia sheepishly and shrugged.

"And then to attack Jake's friend? That's un-freaking-believable!"

"She didn't attack him, Molly. She was fending him off," Jake corrected her.

Molly rolled her eyes. "Whatever. I'm impressed that she did any of this stuff. She's usually so reserved."

Cordelia folded her arms across her chest. They were talking about her like she wasn't even there. How shocking. She was about to give Molly a little attitude, when Jake stepped in.

"Actually, Cordy is pretty spontaneous. She really took me by surprise," he said with a wink.

She wanted him to say more, but Molly was already moving on to another subject.

"So what are we going to do tonight?"

"Well, I thought I'd head out now and let you girls start your summer," Jake said. He put a tinfoil container on the kitchen table, smiled at Cordelia, and mouthed the word *breakfast*.

Cordelia would have ripped it open and chowed down if her esophagus hadn't immediately tightened the moment Jake said he was leaving. As much as she hated seeing him and Molly joined at the hip, the thought of him getting into the Charger and driving away made her feel like she might collapse.

Molly didn't seem to like the idea much either.

"Don't be retarded, Jake. We'd love you to hang around. Right, sis?"

"Sure," she mumbled.

Molly playfully kicked Cordelia in the shin. "What's the matter with you?"

Jake shoved his hands into his pockets and stared at his feet. "Really, it's fine. I should get out of your way."

Molly smirked. "You're not going anywhere until we have your party."

Cordelia was completely confused, and so was Jake. "My what?" he asked.

"We're celebrating your…confirmation!" Molly said excitedly.

"But I'm not thirteen, or Catholic," Jake replied.

Cordelia tried to suppress a laugh, but it was pointless. She couldn't believe it, but she'd actually fallen in love with Jake's sense of humor.

"Well, it's a metaphor. You're taking your first steps into the adult world and we should commemorate it," Molly explained.

Cordelia and Jake both did double takes.

"I'm taking this class called Literature and Religious Theory, okay?" Molly said.

Jake chuckled. "Wow. I never thought I'd hear any of those words come out of your mouth."

"So will you stay? We'll take you out to a club and show you a really good time," Molly pleaded.

Jake took a couple of steps toward Cordelia. Her heart ricocheted off the inside of her chest with each of his slight, yet graceful movements.

"What about you, Cordy? Do you want me to stay?" he asked.

She was mesmerized by the sound of his voice just then. It almost beckoned her to take another chance on him. Maybe there was some way she could get him alone. Maybe there was some way she could get him to stay forever, or at least for the rest of the summer. But when she glanced over at Molly, she could see that her sister was beaming. There was no way she'd be able to justify coming on to Jake when Molly would be circling them like a bird of prey! She'd already stepped over the line of bad behavior once. She couldn't do it again, could she?

Cordelia cleared her throat and hoped that when she spoke, Molly wouldn't be able to tell that her little sister was infatuated with her ex-boyfriend. "If you want to stay, then you should. I don't mind."

Jake frowned as if he were disappointed. "Fine, then."

Molly leaped up and down. "Fantastic! Oh, I know just the place we should go. It's called the Hit Stop. Saturday nights are amazing there. You guys will love it."

"Great," Cordelia said solemnly.

"Lighten up, sis. We have loads of prepping to do! Jake, would you mind if Cordy and I went out shopping? You could busy yourself for a few hours, right?"

"Of course," Jake replied.

Cordelia gulped down a mouthful of anxiety. A trip to the mall with Molly was code for "I need you to listen to me as I ramble on and on about some boy." She had a feeling that her sister had a specific guy in mind, and the thought of talking about how awesome and/or "scrumptious"—Molly's favorite adjective—Jake was would be as painful as tweezing the hairs on her bikini line. Besides, if she stayed behind, she had a shot of getting some one-on-one time with Jake.

"You know, I'd love to, but I really should, like, get settled and—"

Molly wasn't going to hear any excuses. "You're helping me max out Dad's credit card and that's that!"

Jake grimaced as Molly snuck behind the beaded curtain and grabbed Cordelia's purse. "Resistance is futile, Cordy."

She sighed as her sister practically pushed her out the front door and into her silver Ford Focus.

Jake couldn't have been more right. About everything.

Chapter Fifteen

Cordelia wanted to dig her own grave as she watched Molly try on another pair of super-low-slung, tight-as-sin jeans. These were dark indigo Sevens. Molly's ass looked dynamite in them, as they did in the other ten pairs she had discarded on the fitting room floor. She didn't think it was possible that Molly could have gotten any prettier, but Cordelia was being proven wrong with each piece of denim that cradled her sister's curvy thighs. And were her boobs bigger too? Cordelia glanced down at her own chest and suddenly felt very insecure. How could Jake possibly think of her as anything but prepubescent when she stood next to her sister's drool-inducing bod?

Molly checked herself out in the full-length mirror. "These are it, honey. What do you think?"

Cordelia gaped at how the back of Molly's neon pink thong was jutting out. "Whatever you do, don't bend over."

"C'mon, guys like it when girls do that."

"I'm sure you've made it into an art form, Molly," she said icily.

Molly spun around and gave her a wicked look. "What's with you today? You've been cranky ever since you showed up."

She swallowed a witty comeback and lowered her eyes. "Sorry."

"Well, are you going to tell me what's wrong? That's what sisters are for, you know."

"I'm just tired from the trip," Cordelia said while mindlessly fiddling with a stray Guess? asymmetrical tunic tank top that Molly had rejected about forty minutes ago.

Molly slipped off the Sevens, balled them up, and threw them in her face. "You're so full of shit. There's something wrong, I know it."

"I said I'm just tired," she said curtly, and tossed the jeans back at Molly.

"Give it up, sis. Jake already told me," Molly replied knowingly.

A surge of panic seized Cordelia. Her breathing became so labored that she began chanting the words to the Pledge of Allegiance in her head to calm down. "What did he tell you exactly?"

She was hoping that Jake *had* told Molly that they messed around. Molly's demeanor was very amiable (as usual), so maybe it didn't even matter to her. Perhaps she couldn't care less if her little sister was into her ex-flame. Not that it would change the fact that Jake didn't seem that interested in Cordelia.

"He said that you and Paul broke up." Molly perched herself on Cordelia's lap. "I'm sorry, sweetie."

Cordelia gazed into her sister's shining eyes and felt comforted for a minute. Then she realized that Molly still didn't know what the hell was going on. Life sucked on so many insurmountable levels.

"You know, Jake said he was an asshole anyway," Molly said, kissing Cordelia's forehead. "I wouldn't even sweat it."

"Isn't that funny?" she snipped. "Jake called *someone else* an asshole?"

Molly laughed. "Yeah, well, things have changed, my dear. Didn't you notice?"

She squirmed a bit so Molly would get up. "Notice what?"

"Let's start with how scrumptious Jake is," Molly said devilishly.

I'm going to be sick, Cordelia thought. She hunched over and buried her head in her hands.

"It's like I've died and gone to hottie heaven!" Molly exclaimed.

Cordelia snickered. "Oh my God, Molly. Are you for real?"

"C'mon, like that never crossed your mind?" Molly asked.

She knew there was no way she could look her sister in the eye and lie, which is why she stared at her knees. "No! He's...he's..."

"Delicious? Delectable? Yummy?"

"It sounds like you're describing a candy bar," Cordelia teased.

Molly giggled. "God, I wanted to bite his lower lip and gnaw on his neck the second I saw him."

Cordelia was now curled up in the plane-crash position, not that she'd ever been taught how to do it properly. She was just imitating what she'd seen on TV and hoped that it would save her from imminent death; she was certain it was near.

"Hey, Cordy? Maybe you could, like, disappear for a little bit tonight." Molly strutted over to the mirror and gazed critically at her pores. "I was hoping Jake and I could find a cozy dark spot and...get reacquainted."

Cordelia's feet felt numb and she could barely squeeze enough air out of her lungs to respond. It didn't matter, though. Molly seemed to take her silence as a yes.

"Not that I want to get back together or anything," Molly said offhandedly. "I just want to see what kissing Hot Jake is like."

Cordelia wanted to tell her it was better than anything she'd ever imagined. But she just sat there motionless until Molly bolted out of the dressing room with her new pair of jeans under one arm and her little sister's broken heart under the other.

*   *   *

The Hit Stop was just as Molly had described it. Fantastically beautiful people were squished together in a room the size of a broom closet, dancing to the lush sounds of BT and drinking blue liquid out of martini glasses. It wasn't really Cordelia's scene, but then again, she'd forgotten what having fun felt like since Jacob Stein's Infamous Kissing Smackdown. Molly, on the other hand, could never, *ever* forget how to have fun. It was ingrained in every strand of her DNA.

After hours of primping and a misguided fashion makeover, Cordelia had slinked into the club at around eleven thirty, looking like Molly's personal stylist had accosted her. Not only was she wearing a dress that was so short it could double as a shirt, but she was also covered in the entire MAC cosmetics line. She'd tried to hide behind Jake and Molly, but that hadn't stopped the crowd from taking notice of the tiny pixie girl who was hobbling onto the dance floor in a pair of gold Dolce & Gabbana platform strappy sandals. Molly had glued herself to Jake from the moment they'd gotten back to the apartment. Cordelia could barely keep down the California rolls she'd had for dinner as she'd watched how Jake hung on every word that Molly had said. And he'd called *Cordelia* the more interesting one. What a joke!

Molly was sipping a cosmo while shimmying seductively to a pulsating techno beat. "I love this song!" she yelled above the music, the contents of her glass sloshing onto the floor.

Jake leaned in and shouted, "It sounds the same as the last one!"

Cordelia just stood there, unamused and unhappy. A random freaky guy was grinding his hips up against her back, and no one seemed to feel the need to rescue her. Then Molly winked and gave her some sort of hand signal that she didn't really recognize.

What does that mean? she thought. *Am I supposed to steal third or something?*

But before she could figure it out, Molly finished up the rest of her drink and handed Cordelia her glass. "Could you get me a refill, sweetie?"

Cordelia turned around and looked at the bar, which was packed with giddy hoochie mamas getting mauled by borderline sleazeballs. It would take her forever to get through that wall of sweaty bodies, as Molly was all too aware. This was the moment when her sister was going to sneak off with Jake and ambush him with her sex-goddess moves. Cordelia was about to keel over.

Then Jake grabbed the glass from her hand, his fingers gently gliding across her palm. "I'll go with you," he said.

Molly wedged herself between them. "Don't leave me out here all by myself!"

Jake smiled. "You'll be fine." He grabbed the greasy himbo who had been up in Cordelia's backyard business and pushed him in front of Molly. "Here, you can dance with this dude until we get back."

Molly's mouth dropped open so far, Crazy Dancing Guy almost thought it was an invitation to French kiss her. Jake put his hand on Cordelia's waist and guided her through the club before she could see what happened next.

There were about seven or so people between them and the bartender, but Cordelia didn't care how long it took to reach the front of the line. She was pressed against Jake so tightly that she could feel the indentations of his abdominal muscles through his snug T-shirt. She looked up at him and reveled in the way his lips turned up at the corners and how his hair was playfully tousled as if he'd just rolled out of bed.

He leaned in and spoke loudly into her ear. "What do you think of the gel?"

Cordelia grinned when she felt his breath sweeping over her bare skin. "Molly's idea?"

"Who else's?" he said with that irresistible smirk of his. "I look like I belong on the set of *Gilmore Girls*."

"You do not." She laughed. "Wait, hold on, you kind of do."

"I know. That Jess guy." He gritted his teeth. "He's my evil twin."

She laughed even harder this time and mindlessly buried her face in his shoulder. He wrapped his arm around her and rested his chin on top of her head.

"Don't you have that backward?" she asked.

Jake pulled her in even closer. "Cordy, you don't think I'm evil, do you?"

The crowd shifted, and they edged toward the bar a little more. Their gaze was broken for a few seconds and she sighed with relief. She had no idea what to say next. One dumb comment and this insignificant, yet equally wonderful, banter would end quicker than it began.

"You're evil in a cartoonish way," she replied. "Like Gargamel on *The Smurfs*."

"See if I buy you a drink ever again," Jake said, chuckling. "That hurt."

Cordelia knew exactly what her sister meant when she'd said she wanted to gnaw on Jake's neck. She was really tempted to lunge at him, but the crowd moved again and they were pushed forward.

Jake put his hand on her lower back, and it sent a rush of chills up her spine. "Hey, can I tell you something?"

She gulped. "Yeah."

"It's about last night."

She gulped again and reminded herself to inhale and exhale or else she'd faint. "Uh-huh."

"I want you to know that I'm sorry."

Cordelia's eyes widened. This was unprecedented. Jacob Stein had never apologized about *anything* since the day they'd met. He had broken her prized Harry Potter shadow box that had won her second place at her middle school literary fair. He had ruined her best ABC Carpet & Home sheets, using them as drop cloths when he'd painted Molly's room a nice shade of lavender. He had picked on her, inconvenienced her, and driven her crazy for months, and this was the very first time she'd ever heard the words *I'm sorry* escape his lips.

But as much as this meant to her, she wanted him to say something else. Something about how he felt about her.

Jake cleared his throat and continued as they shuffled toward the bar. They were next in line. "I guess I just wasn't prepared and I didn't know quite how to react."

This was all good stuff to hear, but she still wanted to know: Did he like kissing her? Did he wish that he hadn't stopped them from doing more than kissing? Was he constantly thinking about being with her like she was thinking about being with him?

Cordelia wanted to ask all these questions, she really did. But she was so frightened of him backing away like he did on the beach that she said nothing.

Then everything started to seem clear once Jake took her hand in his and clutched it firmly. His palm was damp, and she could tell that he was shaking a bit. His brow was crinkling up and his cheeks were flushed. Cordelia could feel herself inflating like a balloon and rising up off the ground—and she wasn't even afraid.

Jake opened his mouth and began to speak, "Cordy, I think—"

Two hands covered Jake's eyes from behind. "Guess who."

Oh boy.

Molly wiggled herself next to Jake and faced Cordelia. "It took me forever to ditch that bonehead. Thanks a lot, Jake!"

He instantly let go of Cordelia's hand, and she deflated just as rapidly.

The bartender approached them. "What'll it be?"

"A cosmo, a vodka tonic, and…" Jake looked at Cordy, "What do you want, sweetheart?"

Cordelia nearly choked on her own saliva. Did he just call her 'sweetheart'? Right in front of Molly?

"Rum and Coke, thanks," she murmured.

Molly was completely oblivious, though. The little pet name went in one ear and out the other. Once the bartender gave them their drinks and Joel Packer's credit card got another healthy workout, Jake excused himself to the bathroom. Molly took this chance to corner Cordelia.

"Okay, babe. I need to call in a major favor. When he comes back, would you fake a headache and say you need to go home?" Molly asked hopefully.

Cordelia couldn't believe this. *Hel-lo?!* Hadn't Molly heard Jake call her *sweetheart*? Hadn't she realized that she'd interrupted a special moment that could have led to something amazing? Hadn't she stopped for a minute to consider her sister's feelings? No, no, and a resounding N-O!

"Molly, I want to stay and hang out. I'm having a good time, actually," she said.

"That's great, sis! I'm so psyched that you like it," Molly shrieked above the noise. "This is going to be *our* place from now on. And you are going to meet someone fantastic here! Trust me."

She shook her head in frustration. Molly had no clue what was going on and it wasn't her fault at all. Cordelia had to tell her how she felt about Jake or else this was going to turn into a bigger disaster than it already was. She didn't want to spend the summer hooking up with someone else. She wanted *Jake*, and no matter how much that might bruise Molly's ego or cause sisterly discord, she just couldn't live with herself if she hid it for one minute more.

"Jake, there you are!" Molly squealed, and linked arms with him.

What the hell? Cordelia thought to herself. Everyone's timing tonight was *so* messed up.

"All right, bring on more lifeless computer-generated music," Jake said while punching his fist in the air.

Cordelia glanced at his glass, which was almost empty. Apparently, Jake had pounded his drink, hence the fuzzy glaze over his eyes.

Molly grabbed his bicep and visibly trembled in pleasure. "Bad news. Cordy's feeling a little under the weather."

Oh my God, she thought. *Molly is going ahead with this!*

"What's wrong?" he asked in concern.

"Nothing, I—"

"She has a headache. Wanna go home, hon?" Molly interjected.

"Well, no, I—"

"Why don't we just call it a night, then?" Jake suggested.

This was happening way too fast. Cordelia wanted to put on the brakes, but Molly spoke up again. "It's early and you're leaving tomorrow. She'll be fine, really."

Jake looked over at Molly, who was practically nibbling on his earlobe, and then back to Cordelia. "Are you sure you're okay?" There were so many ways to answer that question. But the one that summed it all up was on the tip of Cordelia's tongue.

"No, I'm not," she said.

Molly reached into her purse and grabbed a twenty-dollar bill and a set of keys. "Here you go, sweetie. The guy out front will call you a cab, and there's a ton of Advil in the top drawer of my dresser."

Cordelia wanted to strangle her sister for what she was doing, but she knew Molly well enough to know that there was no malice behind it. She was simply not aware that this even mattered to her little sister. And why should it? It's not as if Jake insisted that he take her home. It's not as if he'd told her that he wanted to be with her and not Molly. It's not as if Cordelia had any right to be mad.

But she was. In fact, she was so furious she couldn't see straight. She snatched her sister's money and the keys and bolted out of the Hit Stop without saying another word. She didn't look behind her to see if Jake was watching her leave. She didn't cry on the cab ride back to Molly's college lair. She didn't stay up past four A.M., even though her sister and the boy she was crazy about hadn't come home yet.

She fell asleep after counting the ceiling tiles over and over again, and deciding that tomorrow she was going back to San Diego.

Chapter Sixteen

Cordelia woke up at noon to a throbbing headache and the sound of muffled laughter coming through the wall. She groggily peered through the beaded curtain and glanced at the small love seat that was on the other side of the living room. Jake wasn't sleeping on it, as he should have been. The linens that Molly had put out for him last evening were still stacked up neatly on the couch cushions. Cordelia massaged her temples as she contemplated the possibility that Jake was romping around in his boxers on Molly's twin bed. When she heard her sister yelling "That tickles!" she nearly suffered a stroke.

Apparently, Molly had gotten her wish. She had tempted Jake with her long limbs and her beautiful complexion and her gravity-defying boobs, and now he was probably straddling her or something.

Cordelia ran to the bathroom and hurled herself over the toilet bowl. The cool porcelain felt great against her hot skin, and although her stomach was cramping, she didn't throw up. Her heart was palpitating and her muscles were quivering. Her mind kept chanting: *Jake and Molly had sex. Jake and Molly. Had sex.*

Maybe I'll just stay in this bathroom for the rest of my life, she thought.

There was a soft tap on the door.

"You okay in there, sis?"

Oh God, Molly. Cordelia didn't think she could deal with her right now. In fact, she'd rather flush herself and let the California sewage system carry her back home.

The doorknob jiggled, and within seconds Molly was hovering over Cordelia. "Oh no! You're puking!"

Shit, I forgot to lock the door.

Cordelia looked up at her sister, who was wearing nothing but an all-too-familiar Pedro the Lion concert T-shirt and a smile. Her stomach grumbled loudly. "Just leave me alone."

Molly tried to hold Cordelia's hair back, but Cordelia swatted at her hands. "I'm trying to help you."

"Well, don't," she barked.

"Someone needs some coffee and quick," Molly said cheerily.

Cordelia's rage was simmering. "I'm fine. Now get out of here, okay?"

"In a second, bitchy-pants. I need to grab something and I'll be out of your precious way."

The urge to purge heightened once Cordelia thought about what Molly might grab. Lubricant? Condoms? Chocolate-flavored body butter?

Thankfully, it was only a packet of Oral-B Brush Ups.

"The taste in my mouth is nasty," Molly proclaimed.

"Are you done now?" Cordelia asked with a sneer.

Molly leaned up against the sink and grinned. "Don't you want to hear about my night?"

Cordelia tried not to gag. "Not really."

"Well, Jake and I—"

Those were the only words that stuck in Cordelia's brain: "Jake and I." Everything else just sounded like buzzing in her ears. She could see Molly's facial expressions and her gestures. She obviously had a night of passion that was worth printing in the letters section of *Hustler* magazine. Then Cordelia spotted a huge hickey on the left side of her sister's neck. She began to feel dizzy and weak when she imagined Jake slurping all over Molly, and within no time, the weakness morphed into searing jealousy, which subsequently transformed into a fury that she couldn't contain anymore.

"Will you shut the fuck up?" she screamed, and leaped up.

Molly was totally taken by surprise. So much so that she just stood there stunned.

Cordelia kept on yelling, though. "Do you *really* think I want to hear any more about how you *did it all morning long* with Jacob Stein? *It's killing me!*"

"What are you talking about?"

"You and Jake's lips and his ass and his eyes and his hands all over you. *I can't take it!*"

"And why not?" Molly said suspiciously, and crossed her arms in front of her chest.

"It's *disgusting*, that's why!" she cried. "So disgusting that I'm going back home."

"Is that so?" Molly asked.

"Yes," Cordelia mumbled, her lower lip wobbling. She was practically in tears.

"Well, it looks like you weren't listening to my story *at all*," Molly said, giggling a bit. "Nothing happened between me and Jake."

Cordelia's breath caught in her throat. "What?"

Molly went on. "Like I said, Jake and I came back here about an hour after you left. Some jackasses stole all the mirrors off his car, and it's illegal to drive like that. I told Jake we could get them replaced today, but he seemed too pissed off to listen to reason. He claimed his car was crap and he didn't have his license on him anyway, so he said he was better off abandoning it and flying out to Seattle as soon as possible. So I took him to the airport and put the tickets on Dad's AmEx. I figured Dad owed him that much for all the shit he went through to bring you here, right?"

Oh my God, he's gone, Cordelia thought. *He didn't have sex with Molly* and *he's gone!*

"Then why are you in his T-shirt?" was all she could think to say.

"I spilled my drink all over myself at the club," Molly explained. "This was layered over his white Hanes one, so he gave it to me."

Cordelia gave into the wave of sadness and relief that she was feeling and began to cry. Molly knelt down and put her arms around her.

"So what's going on—do you *like* Jake now or something?" Molly asked. "That's impossible. You hate him!"

Cordelia just kept sobbing.

"Oh my God, sis. You like Jake! Why didn't you say something earlier?"

She sniffled. "I don't know. I didn't want to hurt your feelings." She sobbed some more. "Anyway, I don't even think Jake likes me back."

Suddenly, Molly laughed really hard. "Are you kidding? He's crazy about you!"

"He is not," she said in disbelief. "I'm a total loser."

"Why are you a loser?" Molly asked.

"Because! I broke that stupid rule! I showed Jake how I felt about him and it backfired and now he's gone and that's why I'm a stupid loser!" she rambled.

"Well, he doesn't think you're a loser." Molly stroked Cordelia's hair lovingly. "Actually, after you left, all he did was talk about how worried he was about you. And when we went to breakfast yesterday, all he did was talk about how great you were and how much you've changed."

Cordelia knew this was true. She *had* changed—not completely, of course. But just enough so that she felt she had that sense of balance in her life, so she didn't feel like she had to rely on schedules or predictability or organization in order for life to seem more manageable and less scary. Jake showed her that when she let some of that go and everything wasn't in her control, things still worked out in the end. She realized that the times when she felt most centered and balanced were when Jake was around to light a fire underneath her, and when it came down to it, she discovered that Jake was similar to her in many ways. And there was so much more to know about him.

But more importantly, it seemed that Cordelia had just as much of an impact on Jake. She wanted this to make her feel better, but instead she felt even worse because now he was hundreds of miles away.

Molly nuzzled her a bit more. "I couldn't have hooked up with him if I'd wanted to, hon. He's completely head over heels for you."

"But why did he leave without saying good-bye? Why didn't he come back here and tell me how he felt?"

Molly's eyes brightened. "Holy shit! *You're* the girl on the beach!"

Cordelia was too flabbergasted to reply.

"On the way to the airport, I asked him why he wanted to rush out to Seattle at the crack of dawn. Then he told me that he'd blown it big time with this amazing girl who he'd kissed on the beach. He said that he'd never felt that connected to anyone and it terrified him, so he pushed her away. I guess he's running for the hills now," Molly said thoughtfully.

Cordelia thought of how she'd avoided the things that scared her most, and she understood all too well what Jake must be doing. Still, it broke her heart to know that she couldn't reach out to him. He didn't have a phone anymore—thanks to her own stupidity—and she had no idea where he was going.

This was the end of the line.

There was another tap on the door. "Everything okay in there?"

Definitely a male voice. With a British accent.

Molly smirked. "We'll be out in a minute, Julian."

Cordelia gave her sister a sideways glance. "Who the hell is Julian?"

"A pilot," her sister said with a deep sigh. "Met him at this airport bar after Jake wandered off to catch his flight. God, Cordy, he was so scrumptious, I just had to take him home with me."

They both erupted into a fit of hysterical laughter.

Cordelia wiped at her eyes. "You never quit, do you?"

"Hey, it's called 'the friendly skies' for a reason," Molly quipped. "Besides, a fling with Julian could be worth tons of perks."

Just then, a bolt of lightning struck a cluster of neurons in Cordelia's brain. "Wait a sec. Can Julian get an important message to a plane that's already in flight?"

Molly knew exactly where Cordelia's thought process was headed. It was rare when this happened, but when it did, it was magic.

They both dashed out of the bathroom and cornered a tall, buff, and gorgeous Julian, who was wearing Molly's yellow bathrobe. They begged him to call a bunch of people who might be able to get through to Jake, and he happily complied. After being put on hold eight times, Julian hung up his cell phone and smiled at Cordelia.

"This is your lucky day," he said.

"Why?"

"Your friend's plane was delayed because of inclement weather. It's scheduled to take off in an hour, so he should still be at the airport."

Molly hugged Cordelia in her excitement. "Julian, what's the quickest way there?"

*　　*　　*

Cordelia feared more for her life now than she had when Paul had forced her on that helicopter at Yosemite. Molly was tearing up Route 101, and each passing car was reduced to a flash of light. Twenty minutes before, she'd gunned the Ford Focus down side streets in town and averted traffic by whizzing along the shoulder of the road. Cordelia was clinging to the dashboard and hoping that she'd make it to Arcata-Eureka Airport intact.

"Molly, are you sure it's safe to go eighty-five here?" Cordelia asked warily.

"Don't get all wussy on me, babe," Molly said while adjusting her fake Gucci sunglasses. "Missing Jake isn't an option."

Cordelia affectionately put her hand on Molly's mega-tanned leg. She was being so great about everything. In fact, it occurred to Cordelia that she hadn't even asked her sister whether or not all of this bothered her.

"Hey, Molly, are we cool?"

Molly took Cordelia's hand and gave it a soft tug. "Oh my God, yes! What, were you worried about me being upset over Jakey?"

Cordelia chuckled. "Remember when I borrowed your OutKast CD and you nearly ripped me to pieces?"

"I was so immature a few months ago," she said jokingly. "Really, Cordy, it's a little weird and all. But it looks like Jake and I are meant to be friends, which is fine. And honestly, I've known him a long time and he hasn't seemed happier than when he's talking about you. God, I wish I was kidding!"

Signs for Arcata-Eureka Airport were upon them. They were almost there.

"I don't think anyone's ever told him how talented he is, Cordy," Molly said as the Focus pulled up in front of the airport entrance. "Not even me. It seemed like it meant the world to him. He's going to audition for some bands in Seattle. He never would have done that before you came along."

Cordelia gripped the armrest on the door in sheer exhilaration. Holding Jake in her arms could be only minutes away.

Molly leaned over and kissed her on the forehead. "Okay, make me proud, girl!"

She rolled her eyes. "Could you be any cheesier?"

"Fine. Get out of here and steal my ex-boyfriend or else I'll kick your ass!"

Cordelia laughed. "Much better."

And then she bounded out of the car. Once she made it through the security check, she sprinted ahead to the main lobby. She looked around and noticed that the airport wasn't very large. Cordelia was relieved— finding Jake in here probably wouldn't be too hard. She scoured the terminal and grabbed a total of five differ- ent guys with dark disheveled hair and T-shirts, but they turned out to be Frank, Bill, Scott, Rich, and Todd—not Jake.

She checked the departures list and saw that there were no direct flights to Seattle. There were a bunch of other destinations throughout California, though. Still, she had no idea which connecting flight was Jake's. She cursed herself for not thinking to ask Julian more info about Jake's flight details. Molly had rushed her out the door so fast that she had barely had a chance to say thank you.

Cordelia shifted into problem-solving mode. She looked at all the ticket counters, but they were swamped with people. So were the information kiosks. Then Cordelia grabbed her purse and rummaged through it until she found her savior.

The Treo.

Although it hadn't brought her much joy lately, she couldn't be happier to see its face. Cordelia typed on the keypad furiously and got online to check out which flights had been delayed at the Arcata-Eureka Airport in the last twenty-four hours. She watched the little blinking cursor turn into an hourglass and waited for the tabulation. There were two—Flight 336 to Los Angeles and Flight 61 to San Francisco. She did a little more researching and discovered that both of them could have connections to Seattle. Then she checked the departures list once again. Flight 336 had taken off an hour ago, but Flight 61 was on its final boarding call at Gate C.

Cordelia spotted it straight ahead of her. She dashed toward the people who were guarding the entrance to the plane's passageway, and of course, they stopped her from getting by.

"Ticket please, miss?" asked a skinny woman with wire-rimmed glasses.

"I don't have a ticket, I just need to speak to someone who may or may not be on this plane," Cordelia said in between breaths. "It'll only take a second."

"I'm sorry, that's against regulations," the woman said apologetically.

"Well, can I write something down and maybe you could deliver it?"

The woman was getting less patient. "They're closing the doors now, miss. And I'm not working as an attendant on this flight."

Cordelia was beside herself. She'd gotten this far, she couldn't possibly get turned away.

"I think you can make an exception this time," a saucy British voice said from behind.

Cordelia spun around and there was Julian in all his gorgeous uniformed glory.

"Trailing your sister's car nearly killed me," he said. Then he waved to the woman, who stepped aside as if to let her by.

She gave him a quick hug and darted down the tunnel that led to the plane. Once she got on board, she rushed down the aisle, checking the faces of each passenger in the hopes that her eyes would connect with Jake's. The flight was only half full, so there were a lot of empty seats. Thankfully, it made everything go much quicker.

It took less than a minute for Cordelia to reach the back of the plane, and Jake was nowhere in sight. Her knees were wobbling so much that she was certain they would buckle underneath her weight. She felt heavy and tired and unbelievably sad. Jake must have been on that other flight, and after all she'd gone through, she'd missed her chance with him.

She was on the verge of bursting into the biggest crying fit of her life, when a loud flushing sound startled her.

Cordelia glanced over her shoulder and saw the person who was emerging from the bathroom and zipping up his pants.

When Jake finally looked up at her, he had a shocked expression on his face—and then he grinned. "Taking a calculated risk, I see."

A part of her wanted to play it cool and a part of her wanted to say something that could only be heard in a Cameron Crowe movie.

She didn't do either. Instead, she just threw her arms around his neck and squeezed him like she was saying good-bye rather than hello. She was deliriously happy that Jake was holding her just as tightly.

"What are you doing here?" he whispered. "You're afraid of vehicles that fly."

"I know," she replied. "But that wasn't going to stop me from not letting you go without doing this."

And with that, Cordelia stood on her tiptoes and kissed him. As his lips gently massaged hers, there was no worry or anxiety—a sense of utter peace enveloped her in a way that she'd never experienced before.

As for Jake, he didn't pull away this time. He just lingered there with her in blissful smooching harmony until an attendant interrupted them and said they were about to take off.

Jake cupped Cordelia's face in his hands and gazed at her adoringly. "Well, now I don't want to leave."

"So don't," she said, grinning. "We've got all summer to do this."

"I think you're incredible," he said, chuckling.

Cordelia kissed him delicately on the chin. "You are too."

"And I think we're moving," Jake said.

She quickly turned her head and saw that the plane was slowly edging away from the gate. An irritated attendant approached and ordered them to take their seats.

Jake ran his fingers through Cordelia's hair. "Are you going to die on me now?"

Cordelia laughed at the absurdity of it all and realized something amazing. She wasn't afraid. Not of the plane lifting into the air. Not of it crashing down to the ground. Not of the uncertainty of what lay ahead with Jake. Not of missing out on life. She was perfectly balanced and centered and pleasantly, surprisingly, in love.

Jake led her down the aisle, and when they got to their row, she said, "Is it okay if I'm next to the window?"

He leaned in and kissed her sweetly. "Yeah, I don't care as long as I'm next to you."

A few minutes later, the plane was finding its place on the runway. Jake gently massaged Cordelia's left leg as he began to tell her about everything that was going to happen during take-off. Cordelia quickly texted Molly on her Treo that she and Jake would be taking a trip to San Francisco, and from there, who knew what would happen? She got a rapid response from Molly that read: YAY U! DONT SPAZ THOUGH. WILL GET U BACK 2 EUREKA VIA DAD'S AMEX.

Cordelia just rested her head on Jake's shoulder and smiled. Getting back was the last thing on her mind, especially when the plane ascended above the clouds and California's beautiful landscape.

Pssst! Wanna know a thing or two about your crush? Here's an excerpt from Hailey Abbott's

THE SECRETS OF BOYS

His eyes gleamed in the candlelight, a slight smile playing on the corners of his mouth. He began to bend his head toward her and she could feel the heat between them. Cassidy was both scared and excited at the thought of him kissing her, but her guilt kicked in before anything mind-blowing happened.

"I have to go to the bathroom." She wriggled away and dodged through the crowd. She needed to talk to Larissa like whoa! Her life was spiraling out of control very quickly, and she hoped Larissa would be able to talk some sense into her before she did something she'd seriously regret.

"Bathroom," she commanded, dragging Larissa off

her bar stool and toward the door with the comforting skirted figure on the outside.

"So what's up?" Larissa asked once they were safe under the fluorescent overhead lighting. She rummaged in her oversize bag for her Lancôme bronzer and momentarily disappeared in a puffy glittering cloud.

Cassidy watched her and tried to compose herself. She realized she didn't even know where to begin.

"They're pretty cool, aren't they?" Larissa asked, taking advantage of the silence.

"Cool?" Cassidy said. She had no idea what Larissa was talking about. Who were "they"?

"Fumiko and Dina's friends," Larissa continued. "That guy Toby with the shaved head did you know he's a professional graffiti artist? And then Mary-Jane, who won't tell me what she does, but I bet it's something really nasty. Do you think she's a dominatrix? She has that vibe. And, like, who actually names their kid Mary-Jane?"

Cassidy couldn't have picked Toby or Mary-Jane out of a police lineup. All she could think about was Zach's face swimming close to hers, the look in his eyes, and that tiny smile.

"I guess so," Cassidy said. "I didn't talk to them much yet."

"You really should," Larissa said. "I mean, Mary-

Jane is fab, but Toby is just . . . amazing. He used to live in San Francisco and build sets. He's totally ripped too. You should check out his biceps if you get a chance."

Cassidy tried to picture Toby in her mind, but she couldn't help seeing Zach and, of course, Eric. Who would be completely heartbroken if he knew where she was, and who she was with, and how she was starting to feel.

"Is he that bald guy?" she asked.

"He's not bald; he just shaves his head," Larissa said.

"I mean, he's like in his early twenties—how could he be bald? You're really out of it tonight, Cass. I can't believe I introduced you to Toby and you can barely remember who he is."

"I'm sorry," Cassidy said. She suddenly felt drained, as if in between wanting Zach and worrying about Eric, she'd expended her allotment of energy for the night. "I guess I'm just a little nervous about the quiz and everything."

Larissa shrugged. "So go home and study," she said, sounding put out. "I'm going to stay here, and then Dina's having an after party at her place since we don't have to open the store until noon tomorrow."

Cassidy waited for Larissa to invite her along like she always did when there was a party, but Larissa just headed for the door.

"Come on," she said. "They're going to think we drowned in here."

"Wait!" Cassidy said. Larissa paused, her hand on the doorknob.

"What?" she asked.

"What do you think of Zach?"

"He's okay, whatever," Larissa said. "I asked him if he wanted my number, but he said he was interested in someone else."

She pushed through the door and back to her friends and Cassidy followed slowly, her head spinning. He'd said he was interested in somebody, but he couldn't be talking about her, could he? Cassidy's muscles tensed up the moment she approached the dance floor and saw Zach waiting patiently for her. He stretched out his hand, beckoning her to join him once more. She took a deep breath and walked forward, hoping that she was the one and almost frightened of what was to come.